The Chronicles of Krangor

The Chronicles of Krangor

BOOK ONE

THE LOST CASTLE

RANDOM HOUSE AUSTRALIA

Random House Australia Pty Ltd
100 Pacific Highway, North Sydney NSW 2060
www.randomhouse.com.au

Sydney   New York   Toronto
London   Auckland   Johannesburg

First published by Random House Australia in 2007

National Library of Australia
Cataloguing-in-Publication Entry

Pryor, Michael.
The lost castle.

For primary school aged children.

ISBN 978 1 74166 204 7

1. Quests (Expeditions) – Juvenile fiction. I. Title.
(Series: Pryor, Michael. Chronicles of Krangor; bk. 1).

A823.3

Cover illustration by Sam Hadley
Cover and text design by Astred Hicks, Wideopen Media
Map by Damien Demaj, DEMAP
Typeset by Midland Typesetters, Australia
Printed and bound by Griffin Press, South Australia

10 9 8 7 6 5 4

For librarians, with thanks

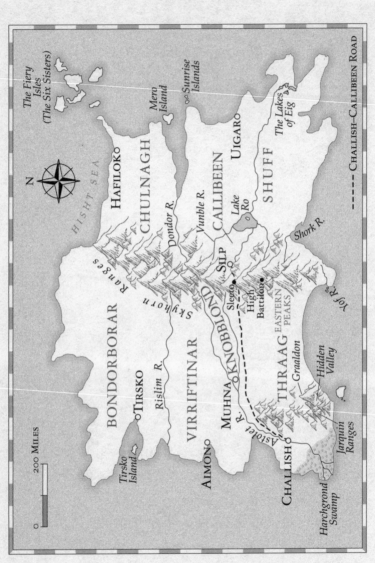

The Seven Kingdoms of Krangor

— — — — CHALLISH–CALLIBEEN ROAD

One

'What do they want?' Adalon asked his father, Lord Ollamon, as they stood behind the parapet of High Battilon.

Sun flashed on the armour and bright blades of the approaching force. The thunder of their passage echoed from the surrounding hills and over the rooftops of Lod, the small village that huddled around the castle's walls.

'I do not know,' Lord Ollamon said, his tail twitching. 'It is strange to see the Queen's Own Guard so far from Challish.'

Adalon's mother had died when he was a baby and he had been close to his father ever since. So he knew

Lord Ollamon was concerned; his claws gripped the stonework hard enough to leave marks. Adalon, however, was eager to see the latest weapons and armour from the smithies of the capital of Thraag. He stared out over the long approach to the castle. The Queen's Own Guard, here in the Eastern Peaks province? It was a wonder!

Adalon had seen fifteen years. He was tall for his age, and strong-shouldered for a Clawed One. He had dashing blue patches on the scales of both cheeks, and his thumb-claws were sharp and curved. Clawed Ones were the swiftest of all the saur kind, and Adalon was renowned for never having lost a race. He tapped his claws on the stone with frustration, waiting for the soldiers to arrive.

Lord Ollamon had assembled a small party in the courtyard. Adalon stood to one side of his father; on the other side stood the courtly Sir Moralon – Lord Ollamon's younger brother and Adalon's uncle. Lord Ollamon greeted the leader of the twenty soldiers.

'General Wargrach,' he called over the sounds of the soldiers' riding beasts, iron shoes clattering on cobblestones. 'What brings you here?'

General Wargrach? Adalon had heard tales of the famous soldier, and he craned his neck to see if the general lived up to his legend.

The general was a short, heavily built Toothed One. Looking at him, Adalon could see the ancestors of the saur, the enormous creatures who strode the world when time was young, making the earth shake beneath their mighty feet. Compared to them, modern saur were small. Better brains had come at the cost of size. Claws had grown smaller as hands learned to grasp. But General Wargrach was a reminder of days gone by. His movements, his bearing, his cold expression – all spoke of the past when the saur were giants.

'I'm here on the Queen's business,' Wargrach growled. He dismounted and waited for his three lieutenants to join him.

'Where are our quarters?' demanded the tallest of the lieutenants, a haughty young Clawed One with shining green throat scales.

'Quarters be hanged,' the other Clawed One

snapped. His eyes were red. 'I need ale to cut the road dust from my throat.' He eyed Lord Ollamon. 'You do have ale out here in the provinces, don't you?'

The soldiers supported this with cheers and shouts as they dismounted their riding beasts. General Wargrach glanced at the third of his lieutenants – a squat Plated One with very dark eyes. He needed no helmet or shield, for his heavy, ridged skin protected him from weapons. His tail had a fearsome spike on the end.

The Plated One plucked a potion bottle from a pouch on his belt. He tossed the violet glass at the two complaining lieutenants. It shattered at their feet and they leaped backward, squawking, as a plume of purple fire licked at them.

The purple flames vanished. General Wargrach held up a clawed hand and the pair stood at attention. 'Inspect the troops. Now.'

They hurried off, arranging the soldiers in two lines and making a great show of checking equipment and weapons.

Adalon was wide-eyed at the casual way the Plated One had used magic. He decided that the general had ordered such a display to impress. It had been successful, for a murmur swept around the courtyard.

Wargrach turned to Ollamon. 'They are young,' he said. 'But they show promise.' He looked around the courtyard and up at the two slender towers that flew the flag of the Eastern Peaks province. 'I have not visited your castle before, Ollamon. I would see more of it.'

'Moralon will show you the castle,' Lord Ollamon said, 'while I make sure your soldiers are well quartered.'

Moralon inclined his head. 'Of course.'

Adalon tagged along as his uncle took the general and his lieutenants on a tour. General Wargrach listened and observed, showing interest in the construction of the castle. The Clawed One lieutenants sneered constantly, and complained about being so far from the royal court at Challish. The Plated One said nothing.

Moralon hurried ahead of the small party, closing doors to untidy parts of the castle. 'I'm sorry,' he said over and over again, 'we weren't expecting you. We were unprepared.'

General Wargrach waved the apologies away. 'Are the stables down here?'

'Indeed, let me show you.' Moralon scurried ahead, much to the amusement of the lieutenants.

It was at dinner that night, in the banqueting hall, that the purpose of General Wargrach's visit was revealed.

Adalon was sitting near the head of the table, to the left of his great-uncle Baradon. Baradon was an enormous Clawed One. In his youth, his bulk had been muscle. Now, his love of food and his lack of activity had turned the muscle to fat. His belly hung over his belt, and he often struggled to rise once he settled himself in a chair.

Moralon was there, and a few of the more important saur from the town were present as well. They were mightily impressed by the uniforms of General Wargrach and his aides.

Adalon listened closely to the arguments and banter that lunged up and down the table. Insults came from General Wargrach's Clawed One aides, and they roared with laughter whenever one of the other guests took offence. They attacked their food, cracking bones in their jaws, grinding them noisily and shouting for more from the servants. The Plated One sat at Wargrach's left hand and ate sparingly, drinking only water.

Adalon found it difficult to make up his mind about General Wargrach. He noticed how everyone listened when the general spoke. His voice was a deep growl, but he never had to raise it. While his aides drank tankard after tankard of ale and wine, the general barely sipped at his. His eyes were hard and cold, and he spent as much time sizing up the banqueting hall as he did studying the others at the table. Adalon noticed that his gaze lingered on Moralon, and it was a gaze full of calculation.

After the meal, Lord Ollamon cleared his throat and tapped a claw on the table until he had everyone's attention. 'General Wargrach. While we are always happy to see the Queen's representative, I'm sure we'd all be interested in hearing your reason for this visit.'

Adalon would never forget the smile General Wargrach gave at that moment. It was his first of the entire evening and it showed his dagger-like teeth. It was more a challenge than an attempt to be friendly.

'The Queen wishes to build a fortress at Sleeto,' he said, his gaze on Lord Ollamon.

Adalon blinked. Sleeto was a tiny village in the highest of the Eastern Peaks, right in the middle of the only pass to the neighbouring kingdom of Callibeen. Adalon and his friends Targesh and Simangee often spent time there, rambling through the rugged landscape, exploring caves, finding tiny lakes that were as deep and clear as the midnight sky. He had spent many hours boating on those freezing lakes, Simangee singing traditional Crested One songs beside him, while Targesh waited on the shore, a true Horned One, suspicious of water.

A fortress in peaceful Sleeto? he thought. His claws bit into his palms. *Never!*

Lord Ollamon frowned. 'Why?'

'Are you not loyal to your Queen, Lord Ollamon?' General Wargrach growled.

General Wargrach's lieutenants leaned back in their chairs, hands dropping to their weapons.

'Of course I am.'

'Then you'll support the Queen's projects.'

'I have always supported the Queen,' Lord Ollamon said carefully. 'What exactly does she ask of us?'

'When the fortress is complete, it will be garrisoned from the Eastern Peaks. From your province you will conscript one thousand soldiers for duty. You will also be responsible for provisions and equipment for the fortress.'

Lord Ollamon stared. 'One thousand soldiers? From the Eastern Peaks? That is madness! That would be half our able-bodied saur! How would we tend to crops and herds?'

General Wargrach put both of his massive hands on the table. His claws were sharp and cruel. 'A loyal subject would find a way to carry out the Queen's commands.'

Lord Ollamon leaned forward. '*If* those are the Queen's commands. You have this in writing?'

General Wargrach hissed and gripped the table. Adalon thought he was about to heave it over. 'I am the Queen's representative. I am her voice. I need no documents.'

'I am the lord of the Eastern Peaks province.

I have the right to speak directly to the Queen on matters concerning my lands. I will travel to Challish and seek an audience with her.'

General Wargrach stared at Lord Ollamon in silence. Eventually he nodded. 'As you wish.' He stood. His aides joined their commander as he stalked toward the door. When they reached it, the general paused and turned. 'They say the hunting is particularly fine in the Eastern Peaks.'

Lord Ollamon did not reply.

Moralon glanced at his brother, then stood. 'It is, General Wargrach. The game is plentiful.'

'Then perhaps you and Lord Ollamon will join my saur and me at dawn? There's nothing like the smell of blood in the morning.'

Two

The hunting party did not return until evening. Accompanied by the entire Queen's Own Guard, General Wargrach galloped into the courtyard with Lord Ollamon's body slung on his riding beast. Moralon rode at General Wargrach's side, pale and shaking.

'A hunting accident,' General Wargrach announced to the crowd that gathered.

Adalon stepped forward. His knees were trembling and his heart felt as if it would burst. He tried to speak, but the words shrivelled in his mouth. 'Uncle?' he said, but Lord Moralon did not reply. Instead, he stared with dread at General Wargrach.

Immediately, Adalon realised that his father's death

was not an accident. His tail lashed with fury and his hand went to the knife at his belt. He took a step toward Wargrach, but a hand fell on his shoulder. He jerked around to find himself face-to-face with his great-uncle Baradon. The fat, old saur pulled him close, pity in his eyes, and whispered, 'Do not throw your life away.'

Grief seized Adalon. Sobs wracked his body and hot tears ran down his scales. He had lost his lord, his father, his guide and his teacher all at once.

'Saur of the Eastern Peaks,' Wargrach bellowed, 'your lord is dead. His heir, Adalon, has only seen fifteen summers; he has not reached his adulthood. Therefore, Lord Ollamon's brother, Sir Moralon, will become your new lord.'

Moralon dropped his head and closed his eyes for a moment before looking up again. He slipped from his riding beast and took the body of his brother in his arms.

General Wargrach grunted and gestured to his aides. The Queen's Own Guard wheeled out of the gate, leaving the saur of High Battilon behind. Moralon stood in the middle of the courtyard, holding his dead brother, and wept.

Targesh and Simangee took Adalon to his room and stayed with him as he sobbed and raged, unable to believe that his father was truly gone.

'Wargrach!' he cried. He paced the room, unable to keep still. 'You killed my father!'

Targesh was sitting on the bed. It creaked under his massive frame. When he nodded, his two great horns bobbed in sympathy. Simangee was on the window ledge, her head on her knees, her tail curled up. Sad sounds burbled from her long, curved crest. 'Your father was always kind to everyone,' she said, tears in her eyes.

Adalon clenched his fists. The furnace of his rage grew hotter and hotter. 'Why? Why did Wargrach do such a thing?'

Targesh spread his stubby hands and shook his massive neck shield. Simangee didn't answer.

Adalon felt like dashing himself against the hard stone walls of his room. Dimly, he knew he should be grieving, but anger was all he could feel.

'Rest, Adalon,' Simangee said. 'You must calm yourself.'

Adalon ignored her and continued pacing, his tail thrashing. 'It must be the Queen,' he said. 'Wargrach does the Queen's bidding. She must have ordered my father's death.'

'Why?' Targesh said, his brow wrinkling.

'I don't know! How could I know?' Adalon wanted to scream. 'She must have her reasons!'

He stopped his pacing. His father's notes. They would tell him what the Queen was planning.

He dived for the door, flinging it open, oblivious to the startled cries from Targesh and Simangee. He raced along the corridor with all the speed of a Clawed One until he reached the room his father used as an office.

The office was cold and empty. Grey light came through the window, falling on the shelves of books, documents and ledgers that his father had needed to govern the Eastern Peaks. A large table, covered with maps and papers, stood in the middle of the room.

Adalon looked at the desk, then at the papers. The answer would be there somewhere.

He scrabbled through accounts and plans, scanning and discarding them one by one, hissing with frustration. He bounded across the desk and flung open the drawers, searching for what he needed.

'Adalon?' Simangee's voice came from the doorway, but he didn't look up. He took a small book, bound in red leather, from the bottom drawer. The writing belonged to his father. Through eyes full of tears, he read page after page of notes about military preparations right across Thraag. General Wargrach's name featured again and again. He was responsible for much: destroying villages, ordering the inhabitants into the mines. Saur were being moved against their will, and Wargrach and the other generals were enjoying the blessing of the Queen as they pressed the unwilling into the Army.

His father was convinced that Queen Tayesha was planning a war of conquest.

From between the last pages of the book, a small piece of paper fell and drifted to the floor. Adalon picked it up. The paper was divided in two, with childish writing on one half and the strong writing of his father on the other.

Adalon stared at the paper, sank to the floor, and remembered.

His father had taught him to write by copying

out lessons from the great tradition that was the Way of the Claw. 'This way, Adalon, you will not forget them.'

He remembered how his father's hand – so large, with razor-sharp claws – had covered his and helped him shape the letters. His father was so gentle that Adalon was sure he was writing all by himself, until his father removed his hand and Adalon's writing wobbled all over the page like a spider on ice.

They'd laughed and Lord Ollamon had patted Adalon on the back. Then they'd continued their study.

Adalon gazed at the paper and his breath caught in his throat; tears sprang to his eyes. *Oh Father*, he thought, and great sobs tore at him. *I miss you so!*

Adalon's friends took him back to his room, where he wept for hours. He cried and apologised to Targesh and Simangee. Most of all, though, he cried for his father and for all the tomorrows they would not share.

When his weeping dwindled and finally ended,

Adalon was left with sorrow and loss. They had not gone away.

Neither had the anger. Not entirely. It was there, and when he looked over the notes his father had made, he saw that he'd been right. The Queen was turning Thraag into a land of war.

His father had written to his many friends throughout Thraag, and had documented Army movements throughout the country. Adalon's anger grew again, but this time it was measured. He had lost his father but now he realised that the saur of Thraag were in danger of losing even more. Someone had to speak out against the Queen and the generals. Someone had to stand up for the ordinary saur before they were dragged into a conflict that would result in death and destruction for many.

In the depths of the castle, where the foundations rested on solid bedrock, Adalon made a vow. He placed his hands on the rock and called on the land to witness his promise. He knew that this was the most binding, most sacred oath a saur could make, but he did not hesitate. He promised that he would stop Queen Tayesha and General Wargrach.

The trembling he felt in the rock told Adalon that his vow had been witnessed and that it would endure as long as the land endured.

Thus Adalon and his friends were set on the path to Challish, the capital of Thraag, and the Throne Hall on the day of the Ritual of Bonding.

Three

'You! Stop where you are!'

The hoarse shout rang across the square. Adalon and Targesh turned to see five soldiers marching toward them. A few passers-by scurried away with frightened looks, disappearing into lanes and alleyways, one driving a pig before him.

Adalon remembered Challish as a happy, busy place. Not anymore. Since their arrival a few hours ago, he'd seen only suspicion, fear and despair. And many, many soldiers.

Adalon addressed the sergeant in charge, a scarred Toothed One. 'Were you talking to us?'

The saur scowled. 'What is your business here?'

'Our business is our affair.'

'Provincial mudhead,' one of the other soldiers muttered, then spat on the cobblestones.

The sergeant showed his teeth. 'Provincial mudhead or not, I think these two will do nicely. Welcome to the Army, lads.'

Adalon narrowed his eyes. 'Leave us. We are not to be trifled with.'

The soldiers laughed. 'Listen to him,' the sergeant said. 'Thinks he's too good for us, does he? We'll knock that sort of thinking out of him, quick smart.'

The sergeant lurched at Adalon and swung a backhanded blow at him. With Clawed One speed, Adalon shifted to one side and tilted his head. Roaring, the sergeant missed, then staggered past, off balance. He turned. 'Teach them a lesson,' he barked at his squad.

Targesh bellowed, lowered his great head and charged. The soldiers laughed at his ponderous stride, and one threw a handful of mud. It slapped on Targesh's impressive neck shield, and then Targesh was on them. He knocked two into a dirty pool where they floundered and cursed.

Adalon rose on his toes, balanced on his tail for an

instant and bared his teeth. Then he sprinted, leaped over them and threw himself on the remaining two. Using his momentum, he cracked one under the chin with his elbow and tripped the last with his tail. As the soldier tried to climb to his feet, Adalon kneed him behind the ear and he collapsed face first into the mud.

Adalon swivelled and faced the sergeant, who was staring, open-mouthed. 'You call these wretches soldiers? You're just lucky my friend had his horns capped.'

Targesh grunted and shook his horns.

The sergeant slid his sword from its sheath. 'No-one mocks the Thraag Infantry. Bite on this, Clawed One!'

From behind came the sound of more weapons being drawn. Adalon glanced around to see that, apart from the angry, sodden soldiers, the square was still empty. He guessed that the local citizens knew better than to linger when the military were looking for a fight. He took a step back, cursing himself for getting himself into such trouble.

Adalon drew his sword and stood next to Targesh, who held his axe in an easy grip. Adalon was not confident. Their weapons were only ceremonial, as they had been on their way to the Ritual of Bonding. While they may have looked bright and impressive, they were poorly balanced and not meant for fighting. He wished he had his real blade, but no dangerous weapons were allowed in the Throne Hall.

He took a deep breath and faced the soldiers. 'We wish you no harm. Let us go in peace.'

'Peace?' the sergeant hissed. 'Peace is for weaklings! This is a time for blood and glory!'

With a roar, he launched himself at Adalon. His comrades came after him, but the Toothed One had only taken two steps when an arrow plunged through his thigh. He pitched forward, stifling a shriek.

A figure emerged from a lane and darted toward them, bow in hand, dropping a bag of apples. 'Simangee!' Adalon cried. 'Over here!'

The other soldiers closed. Adalon faced a burly Plated One who swung a huge mace. He remembered the lessons his father had taught him. He did not engage with the mace. Instead, he leaned back and let it whistle past. When its weight made the Plated One overbalance, Adalon struck his wrist with the flat of his sword. With a grunt, the Plated One dropped the mace. Adalon twisted and then, with the hilt of his sword, hit his foe in the vulnerable spot under the chin. He dropped like a sack of grain.

Adalon looked around to see that two other soldiers had been struck by arrows from Simangee's bow and were sitting on the slick cobblestones, cursing and trying to staunch their wounds. One more was lying stunned at Targesh's feet.

Simangee trotted over. Adalon took her by the arm. 'Quickly,' he said and, together with Targesh, they fled the square, through twisted lanes and squalid alleys.

'Thraag has fallen on bad times indeed,' Simangee said when they finally emerged in the great plaza in front of the royal palace, 'if roving gangs of bullies can accost travellers like that.'

'They were more than bullies,' Adalon said. 'They were recruiting for the Army.' It worried him that the Army needed to go to such lengths to bolster its strength. It boded ill.

They joined the throng moving toward the gates of the palace, but Simangee stopped just as they reached the guards. 'You go ahead, Adalon. I have a task to do.'

'Sim? You'll miss the Ritual of Bonding.'

She shrugged. 'Before Hoolgar went away he left me some cryptic instructions. He suggested I should look in a certain place in the Great Library of Challish. I may not have a better chance than today, when everyone is at the Ritual of Bonding.'

Hoolgar had been a tutor and mentor to Simangee. An ancient Crested One, he was the chief musician and scholar at High Battilon. He taught all the young ones in the castle, but he had taken a special shine to Simangee. A month or so before General Wargrach's visit, Hoolgar had disappeared, leaving no word of his plans or destination.

Simangee cocked her head. 'Targesh. Why don't you come with me?'

Adalon's heart sank when Targesh nodded. 'Good idea.'

They promised to meet up later, but Adalon was forlorn. Even in the middle of the crowd entering the palace, he felt alone.

He feared he would never see his friends again. Perhaps he should have shared his plans with them, but he decided it may be better this way. He didn't want them in danger.

In the Throne Hall of the palace, Adalon studied the host of nobles, merchants, military and commoners assembled for the great ritual. He saw wonder on the faces of those present for the first time. They were the ones staring at the gold and silver torches, the carved wooden beams a thousand years old, the gold leaf around the tops of the marble pillars. Others were admiring the walls, where the history of the ruling Gralloch family was displayed. Shields and weapons were hanging in rows. Forbidding portraits of queens from centuries past loomed from on high. A giant tapestry celebrated the bloody and glorious battle of Jorgath.

Adalon's eyes narrowed when his gaze fell on this tapestry. It showed everything the Gralloch family held dear. Gralloch warriors were crushing their enemies, slashing them into pieces with no mercy. The Gralloch family were Clawed Ones of the most warlike kind. The Way of the Claw, with its thoughtful, calm lessons, was not for them. They ignored it in favour of their own motto: *Strength and Might*. It was emblazoned under the tapestry, a reminder of what the Grallochs valued.

It seemed to Adalon as if all of the kingdom was gathered in the Throne Hall – and many from other kingdoms, too. Costumes were colourful, mysterious, rich, fine or military, as varied as those who wore them. Long-necked Ones peered over the heads of the crowd, aloof and thoughtful. Crested Ones fluted greetings to each other. Billed Ones marched through the doors in swirls of multicoloured silks.

Adalon noticed a knot of generals in bright uniforms. They obviously considered themselves better than the citizens around them; disdain was clear on their faces.

Wrinkling his nostrils, Adalon glanced up at the incense burners on the wall. He'd never liked the heavily scented smoke. He scratched his snout with a claw and sighed. It was probably for the best that his friends were not present. He didn't want them to be involved.

The throne that gave the hall its name was made of stone. Great-uncle Baradon had told Adalon that the stone reached right down, through the floor, thrusting deep into the earth beneath the palace. It had been here since the first queen of the Gralloch family and it had seen many queens, a long, undisturbed chain reaching back to the dawn of time. 'Made from the bones of the land,' Great-uncle Baradon had told him, years ago, when Adalon was brought to his first Ritual of Bonding. His father had been there then, tall and strong, an honoured guest.

Adalon felt a pang, and a lesson from the Way of the Claw came to him: *Do not deny sorrow – take it into your heart*. He took a deep breath and the hurt faded, but not the memory.

The throne was the heart of the land, the symbol of the bond that allowed the family of Gralloch to rule Thraag. Each queen was joined to the land, protecting and ruling it. In return, the land protected those who dwelled there, and granted the queen great magical powers. It was a mystical union, revered for eons.

Adalon once again felt the enormity of what he was about to do.

Great-uncle Baradon often told of the coronation of young Princess Tayesha. Her mother, the old queen, had died and when Tayesha assumed the throne the kingdom was in raptures. Feasts lasted for days, carnivals for weeks, and the joy lasted for a whole year. Great-uncle Baradon had been present at the coronation. Over an ale or two he loved to tell of the beautiful young Clawed One princess solemnly reciting the vows that wedded her to the land.

Adalon sensed that the crowd was growing uneasy. He flexed his claws and stilled his tail, trying to quell his impatience.

A whisper ran through the room. 'She's coming!'

Adalon was glad he'd had a spurt of growth. It meant he could see, despite the saur in front of him: a burly Knobblonder, almost as wide as she was tall. The bony plates on her shoulders jutted up as high as the top of her head and were tipped with gold. Knobblonders loved gold and never missed a chance to display their wealth.

A curtain parted behind the throne. Adalon heard a vast intake of breath.

Queen Tayesha's robes were velvet, the dark grey of stormy skies. Adalon could hear the click of her claws as she walked across the polished stone floor. She paused and stood motionless a moment, head bowed, and then approached the throne.

Adalon found it hard to believe she had become queen when his great-uncle was young. He saw the Queen's age only in a hint of loose skin at her neck where the scales were dull and tired. Her back was straight, her eyes were clear, her movements were smooth and confident. Her claws were sharpened and polished black. The only Clawed One house to rule in the seven kingdoms, the Grallochs fancied themselves as superior to the Toothed One rulers of Chulnagh, or the ponderous Long-necked priest kings of Bondorborar, or any of the other ruling families.

His heart beat faster as the Queen surveyed her subjects. 'I stand before you,' she said, 'as your ruler and as the partner of the land.'

The assembly relaxed at the familiar words. This ritual had been repeated countless times. To those assembled it was security and continuity, the ongoing bond with the land that sustained them.

Adalon was in turmoil. He felt the security of the words, but he could not forget what Queen Tayesha and General Wargrach had done – and were doing – to the saur of Thraag. *Can I do this?* he wondered. *Am I strong enough?*

The Queen placed her hands together. 'When I became the ruler of Thraag, the land became my partner. Today, I reaffirm that bond. The House of

Gralloch is dedicated to preserving and maintaining the land. In return, the land of Thraag keeps and nourishes us. As it was, and will be.'

'As it was, and will be.' The hall echoed with the mass response. The bass rumbles from the throats of Plated Ones and Horned Ones, the nasal flutings of the Crested Ones, the booming of the Long-necked Ones – all combined to create a chorus that was the sound of the saur people.

'At the dawn of time, the ancestors of the saur were creatures of gigantic size and limited intellect,' the Queen continued. 'As the ages passed, the saur changed, grew smaller, grew wiser, with hands and bodies that could use their larger brains, until we became the saur of today. As it is, and will be.'

'As it is, and will be.'

The Queen sat and Adalon gathered himself. He could delay no longer. He went to confront her.

Four

Adalon headed toward the front, and a murmur ran through the assembly like wind through treetops. He ignored startled looks as he made his way past priests, soldiers and nobles. A heavy hand landed on his shoulder; he shrugged it off and heard an astonished hiss. His passage grew easier as those around stepped back, alarmed but not willing to interfere. Soon, he had reached the front rank of the assembly.

Adalon tapped a Billed One noble on the shoulder. She grunted and turned, which allowed Adalon a gap to squeeze through. The noble looked puzzled, then thoughtful, but before she could say anything, Adalon had passed.

He stood in front of the throne. He took a deep breath, lifted his head and met the gaze of Queen Tayesha.

'Hold,' she said to the guards. They had been surging toward Adalon, but at the Queen's words they stood aside, reluctantly.

The Queen studied Adalon with eyes like dark moons. She bared her teeth. 'In ten thousand years, no-one has interrupted the Ritual of Bonding.'

Adalon bowed. 'Your Majesty, I have no choice.'

'Who are you, youngling?'

'Adalon of the Eastern Peaks, Your Majesty. Lord Ollamon's son.'

'Ah. Lord Ollamon.' The Queen held up a claw. 'You are a loyal subject of mine, I hope, Adalon of the Eastern Peaks?'

'I am a loyal subject of Thraag, Your Majesty.'

Queen Tayesha frowned. 'You are like your father, Adalon, but you are young. Very young. Tread carefully, I advise you.'

'I am old enough to know my duty, Your Majesty.' He took a deep breath. 'Your Majesty, you cannot proceed with the ritual. You must leave the throne of Thraag.'

A chorus of gasps and expressions of shock came from the assembly. A dozen of the nearest saur rushed forward, tails swinging, claws grasping for the upstart.

'Hold,' Queen Tayesha said again. Although soft, her voice cut through the uproar. The saur stumbled to a halt, robes swirling, armour clashing. Adalon stood untouched and alone.

Queen Tayesha studied Adalon. He knew that his future was being weighed. 'There is much you do not understand, Adalon of the Eastern Peaks,' she said and then addressed the assembly. 'Let him go. He is touched by grief; he knows not what he does.'

Adalon stood firm, hoping against hope that he could dissuade the Queen from her plans. 'Your Majesty, you must not continue with the ritual. Your preparations for war against our friends in Callibeen show that you are not fit to rule.'

Uproar again. Shouts, shock and dismay, cries of 'No!' and 'Shame!' This time Adalon was seized from behind. He tore free and staggered toward the Queen.

Queen Tayesha held up a hand. Magic danced

on her claws, harsh silver light, and the crowd hushed. 'Young Adalon has come into some news, it seems,' she said. 'I had thought to announce my plans after the ritual, but I shall tell you all now.'

She placed both hands on the rough arm rests and bowed her head for a moment. When she looked up her eyes were fierce, blazing with power. 'I have ruled this land for sixty years. Thraag has known plenty and safety.'

The assembly gave a subdued cheer, but Adalon saw puzzled expressions on the faces around him. The Ritual of Bonding had never gone this way before.

Queen Tayesha stabbed a claw at the assembly. 'But when I'm gone? Will there ever be such a time again?'

This time, the response was heartier. 'No!' roared the crowd.

She nodded. 'I have no heir, as you know. What can I do to ensure the future of Thraag?' She raised both hands and the glow of power shone on her claws. 'I will not let this bond be broken, this land grow ill and my saur suffer.'

Queen Tayesha stood. Light rippled on her hands, flaring on the tips of her claws, and Adalon had to shade his eyes against the bright silver fire. This was the power he'd dared to confront? He cursed himself for being a fool.

'There is a way to keep the bond,' the Queen said, 'to hold Thraag together. Ancient texts have told me that I can endure. I can endure and the bond can survive. Thraag can have a queen who never dies!'

Adalon's jaw dropped. It was worse than he'd thought. *She's gone mad.*

Queen Tayesha stood tall, proud and beautiful, a ruler who held the power of the land and the adoration of her saur people. 'The texts have told me: if one saur can rule all seven kingdoms, Krangor can be united under a single, immortal ruler. All Krangor will be as one, the land bonded to one ruler. Thraag will dominate all!'

Adalon straightened. His voice rose over the assembly, clear and strong. 'I hear your words, Queen Tayesha. They sing a song of war, invasion and conquest. I hear death, and loss, and ruin. I see ordinary folk butchered and carrion eaters growing fat on fields of battle.'

Queen Tayesha's eyes locked on Adalon. 'You should have left, youngling.'

She held up a hand. The silver light around it swirled, took shape, and a hail of silver thorns flung themselves at Adalon.

Without thinking, he threw himself to one side then rolled to his feet in time to see the Queen shaking her head at him in sorrow more than anger. 'Farewell, youngling.'

Adalon stumbled, looked down, and saw the flagstones crumbling beneath his feet. Before he could move, a hole opened and the earth swallowed him.

Five

The Needle was the tallest tower in the Gralloch Palace. At the top was a single room. In all the centuries the castle had seen, only the queens of Thraag had ever set foot inside this room. From it, the entire city of Challish could be seen. Further off, the rounded, ancient hills. Beyond them, the broad, rolling plains.

The small room was lined with bookshelves from floor to ceiling, only broken by the single door and four evenly spaced windows. A narrow desk stood in the middle, and here Queen Tayesha sat. She was writing in a large journal made from the finest paper from Shuff, the southernmost of the seven kingdoms of Thraag.

The poor, misguided youngling, she wrote. *So young, and so awry. Could grief have driven him mad?*

She sighed and put down the quill. She had been sitting still too long, recording her thoughts for the day. She needed to move, or her Clawed One energy would boil over.

While she paced she told herself that it was important to keep her journal faithfully. It would matter, centuries from now, when she wanted to reflect on how she had achieved her eternal life.

She glanced at the books on the walls. Some were rich, others battered and water-stained, others fire-blackened. A multitude of sizes and colours, most had been fetched here at the Queen's orders by agents across the seven kingdoms. General Wargrach had presented her with a number of the most important, most useful texts. He declined to tell her where he had found them and she reminded herself to insist that he tell her, one day.

The books had provided what she had sought for decades – the secret to immortality. Bringing all seven kingdoms under her rule was the way.

Queen Tayesha sat at her desk again and wrote.

Seven kingdoms united under one ruler. What could be more proper, more natural?

She paused for a moment and sighed. Ruling all seven kingdoms would not be an easy task, but she was willing to do it, for the good of all the saur in Krangor. One ruler to guide them and look after them. No more jealousies between kingdoms or petty wars over borders. It was a great and noble goal, but one with much heartache and travail ahead.

For a moment she hung her head. Then she took a deep breath and wrote: *I will do whatever it takes to ensure the future of the saur. Only I can ensure this, so I must press ahead.*

A tap came from the door. Queen Tayesha stilled her impulse to spring to her feet and leap to confront whoever was disturbing her. 'Yes?' she said eventually.

The door opened. 'Your Majesty?' Standing there was Lady Sillian, one of her ladies-in-waiting. A flighty Crested One, her hands fluttered in front of her. 'It . . . it's General Wargrach. He wishes to see you.'

Queen Tayesha grimaced. Wargrach had been growing too pleased with himself lately. He was certainly useful, but he would bear watching. 'Tell him to meet me in the Morning Room.'

'Yes, Your Majesty.'

Queen Tayesha listened to the scuttling sound of Lady Sillian's claws descending the stone staircase before she picked up the quill again.

Great deeds require great sacrifices, she wrote. Satisfied with this, she wrote it again. *Great deeds require great sacrifices*.

General Wargrach struggled to conceal a snarl. He'd been ushered into the Morning Room, a parlour with windows overlooking the palace gardens. It was furnished with well-stuffed chairs and sofas from which guests could contemplate the carefully maintained greenery and flowers.

General Wargrach hated chairs. They were a sign of softness, of all that was wrong with the world. He preferred to use his bulky tail to prop himself where he stood.

Years on the parade ground and the battlefield had hardened the General's muscles and he could remain upright like that for hours, always ready to launch forward and attack. Not like the namby-pamby saur he saw around him everywhere in the capital. It sickened him to see the way the saur had become so meek, so comfortable, so *gentle*.

He glared at the chairs and propped himself in the corner of the room, facing away from the view of the gardens. He crossed his arms over his chest and waited. He was a model of patience.

It was patience that had brought Wargrach this far – patience and ambition. He remembered his earliest days in the gutters of Challish, when he had fought and schemed his way upwards. First leading gangs of orphan thugs who roamed the streets, thieving and threatening, then into the Army, where he could use his brutality in the service of Thraag. As he worked his way up, there were those who thought he was a typical Toothed One – brave, strong, but more than a little stupid.

Wargrach chuckled. Most of the saur who had thought him stupid were now dead.

As he rose through the ranks, he endured the thousand slights and insults that any low-born saur had to endure. He bore them – but never forgot them.

Now that he had achieved power and position, he was able to take his revenge. Against Lord High and Mighty Ollamon, for instance.

Wargrach seethed as he remembered Lord Ollamon visiting Challish forty summers ago. The young lord probably didn't see the corporal he accidentally knocked into the mud when he cantered up to the palace on his riding beast. Oblivious, Ollamon had rushed inside to the Ritual of Bonding and left the mud-bespattered Wargrach to suffer the laughter of the troops.

Wargrach never forgot this humiliation. It burned for years before he was able to do anything about it.

He smiled a little as he recalled how he'd slipped the dagger between Lord Ollamon's ribs, piercing his heart, within sight of his own castle. Very, very satisfying.

Now, with that weakling Moralon quivering in fear, the entire east of Thraag belonged to Wargrach. Every lord, every puny baron, owed him allegiance and was controlled by him. He now had power and riches he'd only ever dreamed of as a street urchin.

If he continued to manage the Queen properly,

he was going to have power for a long, long time.

Lady Sillian appeared at the doorway. She put a hand to her mouth, flustered. 'Oh, General Wargrach.'

Wargrach stared at her and said nothing.

Lady Sillian's hands fluttered. 'Her Majesty is here, General.'

She withdrew and Queen Tayesha swept into the room.

Wargrach stood and bowed. 'Majesty.'

'You wanted to see me, General?'

Wargrach nodded and thought carefully before replying. Handling the Queen was a tricky matter, and he needed all his craftiness.

'Forces are at work, Your Majesty. Forces who would deny you your destiny.'

Queen Tayesha hissed and swung her tail from side to side. 'More? I thought you had rooted out the last of them.'

'They are more powerful than we thought, Your Majesty. I will need more troops, more gold to crush them.'

Queen Tayesha pointed a sharp claw at Wargrach. 'You are trustworthy, are you not, Wargrach?'

Wargrach was immediately alert. He was

convinced that Queen Tayesha was mad, but he knew she was far from stupid.

'I am, Your Majesty. Everything I do is to support your aims.'

'That's because your aims and mine happen to fit well together.'

Wargrach tightened his jaws.

Queen Tayesha nodded. 'Don't worry, Wargrach. I'm sure we can keep working together. You help me gain control of all Krangor, and you will have riches beyond your wildest dreams.'

Wargrach bowed again. 'Your Majesty.'

'Now, General. Make sure you put down any hint of rebellion. We must tolerate no resistance in Thraag, no dissent. No matter how pitiful.'

Wargrach bared his teeth. 'Lord Ollamon's son?'

'He's in the dungeons.' She paused, took a deep breath. 'His own words have condemned him. Young though he may be, he is a traitor.'

Wargrach nodded. 'I will see to it that he will not be one for much longer.'

Six

'Wake up, Adalon, we must flee!'

Even though he was still groggy, Adalon knew that voice. He opened his eyes. 'Simangee,' he croaked. He turned his head a little to see the other figure standing over him. 'Targesh.'

Targesh nodded and his horns bobbed in the dim light that entered through a small, barred window behind him. He reached down and helped Adalon to his feet. Simangee took his arm. 'We must go now.'

The cell spun around him, and Adalon clung to Targesh's broad shoulders. 'Where have you been?'

'We thought you might try something brave and

stupid,' Simangee said. 'So instead of joining you, we readied ourselves for a rescue.'

'Rescue? What happened?'

Simangee grimaced as if she had tasted something nasty. 'It's the talk of Challish. The Queen used her power and the land swallowed you. You could have been entombed forever, but she put you here, saying she pitied you.'

'Stinking place,' Targesh rumbled. He kicked at a damp and moss-covered wall.

Simangee nodded. 'I think you would have rotted down here if not for Targesh. He found a dungeon keeper who had served under your father. He was willing to help. Your father inspired loyalty.'

Adalon's heart ached. *Oh Father, what have I done?*

'Here.' Targesh threw a bundle at Adalon. He amazed himself when he caught it.

'A cloak,' he mumbled.

'The guards stole your finery and your ceremonial weapons. We organised riding beasts, and some more equipment,' Simangee said. 'Come. Now.'

Adalon struggled with the cloak. As he did, his head began to clear. He remembered confronting the Queen. He remembered the blaze of power in her eyes. He remembered falling – but that was all.

'Wait,' he said. 'Where are we going? Back to the Eastern Peaks?'

Targesh glanced at Simangee. 'You can't,' she said. 'The Queen has stripped you of any claim to your land, your money and your title, in preparation for your execution.'

Adalon stared at his friends. He felt as if the world had suddenly turned to smoke and was vanishing through his claws. 'All gone?'

'Gone,' Targesh said.

Adalon rubbed his head. 'I must flee.'

Simangee grinned. 'You don't think you're going alone, do you? Targesh and I are going with you.'

'You can't give up your whole life like this. I'm going to be an exile, an outlaw!'

'We're your friends, Adalon,' Simangee said. 'We'll stand by you.'

'Loyalty,' Targesh said and he touched his nose horn. '*Life is loyalty*. So says the Way of the Horn.'

Adalon could not speak. *What have I done to deserve this?* he wondered. *They're throwing away their family, their homes, their prospects, all for me.*

Simangee looked at him. 'It's not just for you, Adalon. You're not alone in opposing the Queen. There are many who feel she has gone too far.'

Adalon pulled the battered cloak around his shoulders. 'You're reading minds now, Simangee?'

'Your face is as easy to read as a book, Adalon.'

He frowned. 'The Queen needs to be stopped.'

'First of all, we must escape,' Simangee said. 'Once we're safe, we can decide what to do about the Queen.'

'We must do something,' Adalon said, softly.

'Aye,' Targesh said. He seemed to search for words. 'It's not right.'

'We are young, but we are strong,' Simangee said. 'We'll gather others around us, rally saur to the cause.'

'But where? I'll be hunted once it's discovered I'm gone. Where can we be safe?'

'Did you think I went to the Great Library on a whim?' Simangee said. 'Hoolgar's hints led me to find a lost book, and it speaks of a hidden place. A place for us to hide.'

Adalon nodded. Locked in a dungeon, he could do nothing. Escape. Hide. Plan. Then Queen Tayesha would regret what she had done.

General Wargrach stood to attention in the Morning Room. He ground his teeth and looked straight ahead.

The Queen was berating him.

'You said you would ensure the safety of me and my realm, Wargrach!'

Queen Tayesha's eyes were flashing as she paced up and down in front of Wargrach. Her movements were quick and jerky, and her tail whipped from side to side. Breath hissed through her teeth.

'Yes, Majesty.'

'But a youngling has defied me and now escaped.'

'Not for long, Your Majesty.'

'I showed him mercy, and he has treated my kindness with contempt.'

Wargrach shifted where he stood. 'Allow me, Majesty. I'll take a patrol and find this traitor. He'll wish he'd never been born.'

'What about the campaign to take Virriftinar? You should be there.'

'It's well under control. When I left, our troops

had surrounded Aimon, their pitiful capital. It has probably fallen by now.'

'Good. And then?'

'To further Your Majesty's plans, I have positioned a division on the Rislim River between Virriftinar and Bondorborar. They will move north as soon as Virriftinar is ours, and their push will be reinforced by the excess battalions from Aimon.'

'And Knobblond? What about it?'

'Knobblond has its special challenges. We will subdue the other kingdoms on the west of the Skyhorn Ranges before moving on Knobblond. All this, of course, while we prepare to move on Callibeen.'

'This is satisfactory.' Queen Tayesha jerked her head in dismissal. 'Go, Wargrach. Do your duty.'

'It will be a pleasure, Majesty.'

Seven

Adalon rode on, his heart growing heavier and heavier. Would he never see the Eastern Peaks again?

Riding for two days through the hills south of Challish made him realise that spring was coming. The worn summits were white and purple from a scattering of ladies' tears and dayflower. It was beautiful, but Adalon longed for the rocky crags of the Eastern Peaks where spring was wild with snowmelt and gales.

Adalon was thankful for the company of his friends. Simangee sang as they rode, startling birds and small game. She joked and told stories and tried to draw Adalon out of his despondency.

Targesh ran alongside the riding beasts with his tireless stride, horns bobbing, his gaze on the country ahead. He looked slow, but he never fell behind. Adalon had grown up with Targesh trotting beside him while he rode. No riding beast was strong enough to carry a Horned One, so they never learned to ride. Targesh often said he didn't have far to fall if he tripped, but if Adalon's riding beast stumbled . . .

Simangee steered their course across the wilderness, consulting a large leather-bound book that reeked of age. Adalon had been shocked when she admitted she'd stolen it from the Great Library of Challish, but she claimed it belonged to Hoolgar, their old tutor, and had been stolen from him in the first place.

Simangee held the book close to her while she rode, and Adalon understood that he was not the only one who had lost things. Simangee had loved learning the lyre, the rebec and the hurdy-gurdy from Hoolgar. She enjoyed learning languages from him, and delving into the forgotten parts of the castle library. She had grand plans to be a librarian, or court musician, or both.

Stop being sorry for yourself, he admonished himself. *Look to your friends.*

Near noon on the third day of their flight, Simangee called a halt. Adalon dismounted and stretched while Targesh took the opportunity to stuff a handful of grass into his beaky mouth. He saw Adalon looking at him. 'Good grass,' he grunted. 'Try some.'

Adalon snorted. Simangee reached past him and took a handful. 'Excellent,' she said. 'Quite marvellous, really.'

For years Adalon had had to endure the taunts of his two vegetation-eating friends. He knew how to respond. 'Why don't you use that bow of yours and snare one of those fat grouse? I'll cook it up, all hot and tasty, ready to share.'

Simangee slapped him on the shoulder. 'That's better! That's more like Adalon. Goodbye gloom, farewell despair! Welcome back Adalon!'

Adalon managed a small chuckle. Targesh clapped his hands and Simangee bowed.

Later that day, Simangee stood in her stirrups, peering at the landscape ahead. Then she swung down from her riding beast and threw open her saddle bags.

'What is it?' Adalon asked.

'Those mountains. That's where we are bound,' Simangee said. She looked up and a small smile appeared. 'You need to listen to a story.'

Adalon knew Simangee's ways, but he was still taken aback. 'Now?'

'I think so.'

Targesh grunted. 'I'll make a fire.'

Adalon tethered the riding beasts to a stand of small-leaved shrubs as Targesh built the fire from wood they'd carried. Simangee brewed tea and soon they were sitting around the coals. Blue sky above, a sea of green grass around them and a soft breeze. It was tranquil and far, far away from the clashing of armies, the sound of trumpets, and dim, dank dungeons.

Adalon lay on the grass and looked at the few clouds hanging in the sky. He felt calm steal his heart and he thought of the promise he had made at High Battilon. *If I ever put down the burden of my vow*, he wondered, *would it feel like this all the time?*

Simangee knelt by the fire. She had the old book in her lap and her tail curled around her knees. She cleared her throat, looked seriously at both Adalon and Targesh, then assumed her storytelling voice.

'The book tells of the Lost Castle in the Hidden Valley.

'Long ago, in the early days of the seven kingdoms of Krangor, lived a race of saur called the A'ak. They did not belong to any of the seven kingdoms. They were a race apart, with a strange language and writing peculiar to themselves – writing that no-one can read today. They lived in a castle stronghold in the Hidden Valley. It was said to be their refuge and place of safety. They only emerged to raid and plunder and make war. No-one knew where they came from or where they disappeared to, as the valley was shrouded by powerful magic.'

'What sort of saur were they?' Adalon asked. 'Toothed Ones? Clawed Ones?'

Simangee shook her head. 'The book doesn't say. It describes the A'ak as bloodthirsty, powerful, possessing strange and deadly magic.'

Targesh grunted. He sprawled on his stomach, resting his chin on his arms.

'What happened to them?' Adalon asked.

'The vast army of the A'ak perished on its way to battle against a combined force from Thraag and Knobblond. The soldiers were crossing the Harchgrond Swamp in winter when a blizzard fell on them. It was the last anyone heard of the A'ak.'

'And their Hidden Valley? Their Lost Castle?'

'Why do you think they call it the Lost Castle, Adalon? It's never been discovered. Over the centuries, many adventurers have sought it, imagining they could find treasure there.'

'And your book tells you where it is?'

Simangee pointed at the horizon. 'The Jarquin Ranges. The Hidden Valley is there, near Graaldon, the smoking mountain.'

Adalon stood, shaded his eyes and looked ahead.

The Jarquin Ranges were the tallest mountains in all Krangor. Their peaks clawed at the sky and even Adalon, who loved mountain heights, felt ill-at-ease as he gazed at their ragged crowns. The mountains there were unscaleable and impassable, wicked splinters of rock thrust up from the roots of Krangor itself.

'A place of safety, you say,' he remarked to Simangee. He thought he could see a plume of smoke rising from one of the peaks. Or was it just cloud?

'That's what the book promises.' She paused, frowning. 'I think Hoolgar told me about this book for a reason, Adalon. I think he saw war coming to our lands, and he wanted me to know of a place of refuge.'

A *place of refuge*, Adalon thought. Somewhere to rest, to plan. Somewhere his friends could be safe. Adalon nodded. 'Lead on, Sim.'

Targesh frowned. He placed one hand flat on the ground and held it there for a moment. Then he snorted and climbed to his feet. 'Riders,' he said.

Adalon whirled. In the distance he saw black specks against the green of the grassy plains. Dust rose in their wake and he knew they were coming fast. 'They're after us.'

'How d'you know?' Targesh asked.

Adalon gazed into the distance. Targesh had a point.

'We need a scrying spell,' Simangee said.

'I have one,' Targesh said. He held up a small vial, half-full of blue liquid.

'I'm glad *you* do.' Simangee grinned at Adalon. 'I know better than to expect *him* to have a spell.'

Adalon scowled, tilted his head and glared at the vial through one eye. He mistrusted magic. He didn't like its habit of turning on the saur who used it, like a badly-balanced knife. The cost of using magic was unpredictable. It could be petty, but it could be dire.

His friends thought his suspicions were simply a foible, a quirky aspect of his character. He'd never told them that his mother had died from magic gone wrong.

Targesh shrugged his enormous shoulders. 'Thought a spell could be handy.'

Simangee took the vial. 'Thank you, Targesh.'

'*Stand by your friends*,' Targesh said. 'The Way of the Horn.'

Targesh held to the Way of the Horn with deep-seated strength. Adalon knew the Way of the Horn had come down through the ages from the days when the great Horned One herbivores relied on the safety that came from the herd. The mass of the herd protected the young and the weak from Toothed Ones and other dangers. Loyalty, steadfastness and courage were vital to survival, and these qualities were the foundation of the Way of the Horn.

Targesh was a living, breathing model of the Way of the Horn. Faithful, strong, dependable, he was the rock the three friends built their friendship on.

'Quickly, now,' said Simangee. 'We need a pool, or a mirror, something we can see into.'

Targesh frowned. 'None around here.'

'I have a beaker and a canteen of water,' Adalon said. 'Will that be enough?'

'I hope so,' Simangee said.

Once the beaker was full of water, Adalon handed it to Simangee. She uncorked the tiny bottle and tilted it toward the beaker.

Blue liquid fell, as bright as the summer sky at noon. Suddenly the beaker was full of soft light.

Simangee discarded the empty bottle and held up the beaker. 'The riders,' she said clearly, then she lowered the beaker so the others could see.

'General Wargrach,' Adalon said. His heart lurched and his tail whipped from side to side until he stilled it with an effort.

'How many with him?' Targesh asked. He shook his neck shield.

'Twenty or so,' Adalon said. 'Enough.'

Simangee stood. 'We have a head start. They'll have to catch us.'

Eight

Grassland gave way to a broken country of ravines and dry watercourses. Pausing on a small rise, Adalon despaired at the sight of league after league of shattered stone and tumbled boulders. Beyond it lay the Jarquin Ranges and Graaldon, the smoking mountain.

Without a word, Adalon, Simangee and Targesh set off, plunging into the mazy wilderness of stone.

A day later, they were still picking their way between rocky outcrops. Adalon's tail ached, despite his well-made saddle. He felt a chill as clouds darted across the face of the sun. To add to his discomfort, the wind was skating down from the mountains in the south, and it had ice in its teeth.

Gloomily, Adalon thought the boulders around them were beginning to look like skulls.

He was unaccustomed to such prolonged riding, and it irked him. Targesh seemed content enough, jogging alongside the riding beasts. Simangee was able to amuse herself by singing. Sometimes her voice was barely a murmur, but at other times it echoed from the rocks. The lessons of the Way of the Crest were taught through music, and Simangee sang many tunes that made sense only to those who followed this Way. Some tunes were happy and light, some thoughtful and measured, while others baffled Adalon entirely.

He grimaced, adjusted his tail, then sighed. He longed to leap from the saddle and stretch all his muscles. He wanted to run through the rocks, weaving between them until he felt the wind in his face, but he dared not leave Simangee and Targesh. He scratched under his collar and squirmed in his saddle. His tunic was chafing on his shoulders, but no matter how he tried, he couldn't reach the itch with his claws.

Simangee laughed at him. 'Patience, Adalon! When will you learn patience?'

'Ach!' he said. 'How do you stay in one place for so long?'

'Strength of mind, Adalon. Some saur have it, others do not.'

Simangee smiled and he forced a weary chuckle.

As they pushed on, he became increasingly concerned about their pursuers. At midday on the fifth day of their flight, he called a halt. They pulled up near a boulder as large as a house. 'Wait here.'

'What is it?' Simangee asked. Targesh looked questioningly at him.

Adalon pointed at the boulder with one claw. 'We need to know how close General Wargrach is.' He winked. 'Besides, a climb will be good for me.'

'Look for Graaldon,' Simangee urged. 'Among all these rocks, it's hard to be sure we've kept the right heading.'

Targesh took the reins of his riding beast. Adalon ran and leaped at the rock. He dug in with his hand-claws and foot-claws and swarmed up its face, grinning. It was good to be doing something other than riding.

In seconds he reached the rounded top of the boulder. He stood and stretched, then he shaded his eyes and looked toward the mountain range ahead.

'We're almost at the foothills!' he called.

'The smoking peak,' Simangee shouted. 'Can you see it?'

It was hard to miss. Smoke rose from Graaldon in a steady plume. 'Yes, we're close. Half a day, maybe!'

Adalon turned and gazed in the direction of their pursuers. They were only an hour or so behind. He could make out a score of individual riders and saw the sun glinting on weapons. Then his gaze fell on a dozen or so smaller shapes loping alongside the riding beasts. He felt his mouth go dry.

Warhounds.

His father had once had a pack of warhounds. Evil, bloodthirsty, furred beasts, they were a nightmare to control. They had turned on and killed their handler when Adalon was small. His father had them put down after that.

Warhounds were renowned for their tireless pace. Once set loose, the prey was doomed.

Wargrach! Adalon shook a fist at the pursuers. *Haven't you done enough to my family already?*

He turned and scrambled down the rock faster than he went up it. 'We must fly,' he panted when he reached the ground. 'Wargrach and his soldiers are close behind. They have warhounds.'

Targesh's nostrils flared and he gave a throaty rumble. 'Warhounds.' He spat on the ground.

'We must find the entrance to the Hidden Valley,' Simangee said. 'We'll be safe there.'

Adalon frowned. He knew how fast warhounds could run once they were released. He took the reins from Targesh. 'We'll go quicker if we lead the riding beasts.'

He led the way. His knees and elbows struck rocks as he hurried through narrow passages between boulders. He sprang over stones and peered ahead for a path.

His riding beast baulked as the ground grew more uneven and difficult. Adalon had to use all his skill to keep it from stopping. He muttered constantly, urging it along, and tapped its flanks with a claw when it baulked.

An hour on, Adalon was stopped in his tracks by a wall of rock, a jumble of huge boulders blocking the way. 'Back,' he said wearily. 'There's no way forward here.'

Targesh was bringing up the rear. He grunted. Simangee put her head against the flank of her steed and closed her eyes for a moment.

A ghastly howl rose over the rocky landscape, echoing among the boulders. Adalon stiffened.

'Warhounds. They're loose,' Targesh said.

Simangee scanned the area, rising on her toes, her crest swaying anxiously. 'Which way do we go?'

Adalon looked back. 'To those two rocks. I'm sure there's a way around them, and then we'll be heading in the right direction.'

The riding beasts were tired and they resented turning around. They snorted and danced on the spot. Simangee spoke softly to hers, trying to calm it down as the screams of the warhounds came to them again. Adalon clamped his teeth together and flexed his claws. The warhounds' cry set his heart pounding. He found that he was rising on his toes, ready to run or fight. *Steady*, he told himself, and he heard the words of the Way of the Claw. *Do not run the race before it begins.*

'They're getting closer,' Simangee said.

'You're right.' Adalon sighed. 'We must find a place to make a stand.'

Targesh pulled his axe from a strap on his back. He shook his neck to loosen the muscles, then removed the caps from his horns. 'Let them come.' He swung his axe and smiled.

Nine

General Wargrach ran through the stony wilderness, his chest hurting, his muscles burning. His teeth were bared in a fierce grin as he imagined getting his claws on the throat of Ollamon's son.

Wargrach had to admit he was no longer the young saur he used to be. His hand-picked soldiers were younger, fresher, less battle-scarred. But he was not about to let them see him labouring.

He promised himself that Ollamon's son would pay for leading them through this cursed rocky wasteland. He leaped from a flat boulder to the ground then scrambled over a jumbled fall of stone.

A few hours earlier, Wargrach had ordered the

troops to leave the riding beasts behind. He knew they could run faster than they could lead beasts through the rocky maze. His troops had muttered about the waste of fresh meat but had not dared to disobey the great General Wargrach.

'Sir!'

A tall saur leaped up and Wargrach recognised Dorgan, the chief warhound handler. Wargrach stopped and glared at him. It gave him some pleasure to see the youngster panting and holding his side. 'Sir!' Dorgan said. He paused, caught his breath, and propped himself up with his tail. 'The warhounds! They've seen the prey. The handlers are having trouble holding them back!'

Wargrach cocked his head. As he did, the rest of the troop caught up with him. Try as they might, they could not hide their struggle for breath. Several bent at the waist, sucking in huge lungfuls of air.

'Good,' he said to Dorgan. The handler eased his stance, then Wargrach narrowed his eyes. 'The warhounds. They'll leave the prey alive?'

Dorgan shifted on his tail. 'I . . . well . . .' He swallowed. 'Warhounds are difficult, sir. I can't be sure what they'll leave.'

Wargrach bared his teeth. 'You should hope they leave enough for me.'

Adalon tried to remember the lessons his father had given him, how to lead troops and help them overcome their fear. He tried to recall the words of the books he had read, full of famous battles and great heroes.

I wish a few of those heroes were here, he thought as he scanned the ground ahead for the best defensive position.

Pursued by a general in the Queen's Army. Warhounds on their trail. No home to return to. None of it seemed real. What was real was his pounding heart and the way his tail wouldn't keep still.

He glanced at Simangee and Targesh. Simangee's face was determined. Targesh was swinging his axe, his feet planted solidly on the ground. Adalon knew of Targesh's skill with weapons through their hours of practice and mock battles together. He was glad to have him by his side.

He sought comfort in the Way of the Claw, but

the lessons skittered away from him.

They followed the rough path around a large boulder. A high shelf of rocks rose on one side of the path and on the other a stream clattered down the hillside. 'Here,' Adalon declared. 'This is the place.'

Targesh looked around then nodded. 'Yes.' Simangee and Adalon tethered their riding beasts to a straggly bush.

Adalon unsheathed his sword. It was battered and heavy and its blade was spotted with rust. Adalon sighed and remembered the fine steel blade that had been his fifteenth birthday present.

'Don't look so disgusted,' Simangee said sharply. 'We didn't have much time before we fled Challish. We were lucky to find anything.'

The howls came again, closer this time; the riding beasts snorted and stamped. Adalon drummed his claws on the flat of his blade. It rang. 'They'll come around the boulder. You and I will use the bow for as long as we can, Sim. When they close in, I'll change to the sword. You stand behind Targesh and me and keep shooting over our shoulders.' Targesh was no archer, because of his large neck shield. He'd always made fun of bows, but Adalon knew he'd be grateful if the arrows could bring down a few warhounds before they closed.

'You have a sword, too?' Adalon asked Simangee.

'Of course.' She slapped the scabbard by her side. 'It may be light, but it should do the job. If they get past you two.'

'They won't,' Targesh said.

Adalon selected two dozen arrows and jammed them into the earth in front of him. He took his shield and propped it on a rock to his left with his sword.

Simangee clicked her tongue nervously. 'I'll make a song about this, once it's over.'

If we survive, Adalon thought, but did not say aloud.

Targesh pointed. 'They come.'

A dozen long, skinny animals came bounding around the rock toward them. Adalon shuddered at their dead grey hides and their slavering jaws. Needle teeth filled their mouths. Their eyes were small, red-rimmed and squinty. *Ugly*, he thought, and he gripped his bow tighter.

When the warhounds saw their prey a fresh

chorus of howls went up, rising and changing pitch until the sound raked at the air. 'Ready,' Adalon said, and was pleased that his voice was steady. 'Now!

The bowstring snapped past his cheek. As soon as the arrow was on its way, Adalon had nocked another and was picking a target. A shrieking yelp and one of the leading warhounds tumbled and didn't get up. Adalon grimaced when its packmates simply trampled it. One paused an instant to snatch a bite from the fallen hound's neck. Adalon steadied and loosed an arrow that took the hungry brute right in the throat.

Simangee was matching Adalon shaft for shaft. She didn't miss.

Adalon had time for three more arrows before the leading warhounds were on them. Targesh stepped forward, swinging his axe and bellowing. He took down two on the forestroke, and another on the backswing. One warhound, braver than the rest, flung itself at Targesh, who lowered his head, caught the beast on one horn and swung it high into the air. Adalon dropped his bow and whipped out his sword just in time to thrust it over Targesh's axe and impale a wild-eyed horror that was trying to get to his friend.

Targesh grunted and kicked, freeing his axe. Soon, he was swinging his weapon like a scythe through grass. Adalon dragged his sword from the body of the warhound and slashed as another sprang at him. It screamed and Adalon turned, slapped it aside with his tail, then slit its throat with his thumbclaw. Behind him, Simangee's bow was humming. 'Beware!' she cried. 'More!'

Around the boulder swarmed the main pack of warhounds. *A score, thirty, maybe more*, Adalon thought numbly. His sword arm was already aching. He sheathed his gory blade and seized his bow again. As fast as he could, he sent arrows winging toward the horrible, slavering beasts. He tried to be as accurate as Simangee, who brought death with each shaft.

As this next wave of warhounds surged toward them, Targesh held his axe in one hand and heaved stones, aiming to break skulls and legs.

Too soon, the pack was on them. Adalon used his shield as a weapon, crashing it against the narrow heads of the beasts, stunning them until he could use his sword. The world became a blur of snarls, screams, thrusts, hacks and blood.

All the while, Simangee sent shaft after deadly shaft over Adalon's shoulder. The mound of dead warhounds grew in front of them.

A drooling pair of jaws lunged at Adalon and he rammed the shield edge upwards. Then he slashed the hound's neck with a handful of claws.

'Fall back,' Simangee gasped. 'More coming!'

Ten

Bellowing, Targesh shook his neck shield. Blood dripped from his horns as he brandished his axe. At this formidable sight, the warhounds paused, slinking low to the ground and snarling. Their ears were laid back and great, ropy threads of drool hung from their jaws.

Together, Adalon and Targesh shuffled backward.

'Can you hold for a moment?' Simangee asked.

'Yes,' Targesh growled.

Adalon panted and leaned on his shield. His shoulders were aching. The sword hung heavy in his hand. *This is battle? This isn't what the stories tell of!* he thought. *Where's the glory? The adventure?*

He shook himself and suddenly understood that stories weren't always about the truth. *Tell the truth about battle*, he thought, *and no-one would ever want to be a warrior.*

'Good,' said Simangee. 'I think it's time for a spell.'

'You have spells?' Adalon almost turned around, but at that moment the warhounds growled. It was a deep, throaty noise that was full of hunger and desire. There was no mercy in that sound, no pity at all.

The leaders of the pack crouched low and started to creep forward.

'I kept some for emergencies,' Simangee said. 'I believe this is such a time.'

Adalon heard the sound of glass clinking on glass. Then something flew over his shoulder and arced toward the warhounds.

'Get down!' Simangee cried. She dragged both Adalon and Targesh to the ground.

Adalon landed painfully on his tail and his elbow cracked on a flat stone. He hissed with pain and his head jerked up.

The spell vial smashed in front of the warhounds.

Its shattered remains glittered in the sun like jewels, but Adalon's stomach turned at what was rising from the shards.

It was a greasy cloud the colour of spoiled milk. It swelled and grew, writhing as if it were in pain. To Adalon's eyes it looked diseased. He wasn't surprised it smelled like rotten meat.

'What is it?' he gasped. Targesh spat on the ground and rumbled in his chest.

'I don't know,' Simangee said. 'I found the vial lodged behind some books Hoolgar sent me looking for in the library at High Battilon. It said, "Danger". I thought it was for use *against* danger.'

The warhounds were cringing. Their bellies low to the ground, they tried to slink away from the greasy cloud. It quivered and Adalon thought it was looking more solid. Some of the warhounds whined.

'I don't like that thing,' Adalon said. 'But it has the warhounds' attention. Let us go while we can.'

They scrambled to their feet. As they did, the cloud drew itself up in front of the warhounds. With a horrible croaking sound, it fell on the cowering beasts.

'To the riding beasts!' Adalon cried and he knew that, as long as he lived, he would never forget the shrieking sound the warhounds made at that moment.

He sheathed his sword and pushed his friends ahead of him. Behind him, the howls of the warhounds turned to sharp, despairing yips. They cut off one by one until a final, gurgling squeal was left. Then it, too, stopped.

When they reached the riding beasts, Adalon risked a glance back.

The stinking cloud had grown into a tall, conical shape, swaying and twisting over a patch of bright red earth. There was no sign of the warhounds.

What is that thing? Adalon wondered. He knew it was magic, but it was magic of a foul and desperate kind. Looking at it upset him deeply. It was unnatural, *wrong* in a way that offended his very soul.

The cloud stopped its swaying. Across the distance separating them, Adalon was sure that the cloud was looking at him. He felt sick as its gaze slid across him; it was as if something unclean had crawled across his face.

He blinked and hissed. The cloud was coming toward them!

Adalon strapped his shield onto the saddle, then seized the reins of his riding beast. 'Faster!'

Targesh and Simangee were hurrying ahead, urging and leading her riding beast, but they turned at the fear in Adalon's voice. Their eyes opened wide as they saw the cloud rolling toward them with the speed of a summer storm.

Adalon ducked and the cloud whipped past him and toward the others. His riding beast reared and squealed. Targesh cursed but the cloud seemed to ignore him. Instead, it surged at Simangee.

'Sim!' Adalon cried. He watched, helplessly, as the cloud launched itself at his friend. But before the stinking thing reached her, it swerved and shot skywards faster than an arrow. Adalon was thanking the stars but as it flew past Simangee it lashed out, striking her upraised hand.

The cloud raced into the sky, growing smaller and smaller as it went. Simangee stood, holding one hand in the other. She looked puzzled, deep in thought.

Adalon gave the reins of his riding beast to Targesh and went to Simangee's side. 'Are you hurt?'

'Foul thing,' Targesh said.

Adalon put a hand on Simangee's shoulder. As soon as he did, her eyes closed and she collapsed.

Adalon caught her just as she fell. Targesh hurried over and together they eased her to the ground. Targesh looked at Simangee, then at Adalon, concern and worry on his face.

'Hand me the water bottle, Targesh,' Adalon snapped.

Adalon lifted the bottle to Simangee's mouth. Her eyes still closed, Simangee swallowed a little of the water. She tried to bat the bottle away, and she mumbled a few sentences in a language Adalon had never heard before. The sound of it made him shudder.

Targesh looked up. 'Wargrach. He can't be far behind.' He stood and went to the riding beasts.

Adalon gently shook his insensible friend. 'Sim! Wake up! We must go!'

Simangee opened her eyes. Adalon hissed and drew back at what he saw.

Simangee closed her eyes, sighed, and opened them again. 'Adalon.'

'Welcome back,' Adalon said. His voice was shaky and he studied her face. *It's her*, he decided.

He felt his claws digging into his palms and realised he was afraid.

When Simangee had opened her eyes the first time it was as if something else was behind them. Cold and distant, it had stared at Adalon as if he were a tiny, unimportant thing. *Old*, he thought, *whatever it was, it was old*. He shuddered again and covered it up by fussing over Simangee, patting her, feeling the scales on her forehead, insisting that she sip from the water bottle. While he did all this, he peered at his friend, looking for the intruder that he'd glimpsed in her eyes, but all he could see was a confused and frightened Simangee.

'Is it gone?' she asked as Adalon helped her stand. She swayed and he steadied her. He didn't like the way her arms hung limply nor the way her tail didn't support her when she sagged.

'Yes,' he said. 'Whatever it was. It flew away to the east.' He looked to the sky again and wondered if he had spoken the truth. *Simangee*, he thought, *what have you let loose?*

'It was evil,' she said. 'Something from long ago, formed of mighty magic.' She trembled. 'I felt as if I was screaming but no-one could hear me.'

'It's gone now,' Adalon repeated. 'We must go. General Wargrach and his troops aren't far away.'

'Lead on. I'm well enough.'

Eleven

General Wargrach was torn. Should he take the time to hunt down that misbegotten, incompetent warhound handler, or should he simply lead his soldiers after Ollamon's son and his friends?

Wargrach stood on a flat rock the size of a banqueting table. His anger rumbled in his chest, but his outward demeanour was calm. He propped himself on his tail and crossed his arms while he considered what to do. The troops stood at attention at the base of the rock, waiting nervously for his decision. They all looked as if they were glad they weren't Dorgan.

The warhounds had failed. Wargrach and his troop had found some dead, killed by the younglings, but not all. The rest of the pack had disappeared. Wargrach thought it most probable that the warhounds were poorly trained and had gone in pursuit of game.

Dorgan was no fool. He'd known that the warhounds had been unsuccessful. He'd also known that he would be held responsible for their failure. He'd managed to slip away from the troop. No-one had seen him for some time.

Wargrach smiled coldly. The handler was probably miles away by now.

'Forget the warhounds,' he said to his troops. 'We hunt our prey by ourselves.' He glared at all of them. 'I chose each one of you. Do not let me down.'

He lurched forward and clashed his jaws together once, twice, then he threw back his head and roared, filling the air with the hunting cry of a great Toothed One. He felt the blood sing in his veins.

'Now,' he said to his saur. They stared at him with awe. 'Let us run.'

Adalon went first, picking their route as best he could through the never-ending boulders. Targesh marched next to Simangee, supporting her when she struggled. Adalon saw how her head drooped, but whenever he caught her gaze it was fierce and determined. 'We'll get there,' she said. 'I'm sure of it.'

'Sing,' Targesh urged. 'You'll feel better.' She shook her head.

As the sun began to sink lower in the sky, Adalon could see Graaldon, the smoking mountain, getting closer, growing larger all the time. Sometimes, the ground trembled beneath their feet and the riding beasts danced nervously. Overhead, the plume of smoke trailed across the sky, staining it a dismal grey.

After hours of slow going, they came to the foothills, and the stony wilderness began to slope upwards. Adalon was pleased and called a break. Simangee lay on the ground, her eyes closed and her head in her hands.

Adalon was concerned. Simangee's quiet plodding was unlike her. Her singing and her cheeky grin had vanished. Her scales were dull around her eyes, and her shoulders sagged.

He felt guilty and lowered his head. *If it were not for me*, he thought, *Simangee would be safe at High*

Battilon, finding interesting books in the library or making new music.

Adalon sought for guidance in the lessons of the Way of the Claw. He closed his eyes. He breathed deeply and slowly. Gradually, he could hear his father's voice reciting the lessons.

'*A Clawed One is a creature of motion, made for action. Therefore, watch, listen and learn before acting, lest you leap off the edge of a cliff in your haste.*' Adalon smiled as he remembered his father's habit of tapping the side of his jaw with one claw when he was commenting on the lessons. 'This is one of the great lessons of the Way of the Claw,' he had said. 'We Clawed Ones are prone to rush ahead, to spring into conflicts before understanding them. The wisdom of the Way of the Claw is there to temper the impulsiveness we feel in our blood.'

Adalon sighed. He vowed to watch Simangee closely.

While they handed around the water bottle he rubbed his feet. The rocky wilderness was spread out below them and Adalon looked at the maze they had worked their way through. Outcrops of broken stone stood among countless rounded boulders.

Like a giant's toys, Adalon thought. *Left strewn where they fell.*

Movement caught his eye. 'Targesh,' he said. His friend was sampling the thin leaves of a bush that had found a hold between two rocks. 'Is that them?'

Targesh shaded his eyes with his claws. 'Aye.'

Adalon looked anxiously at the sky. 'We've not much light left. Can we go on?'

Simangee lifted her head, her bony crest bobbing. 'Yes. We must.'

Faint shouts drifted up to them. 'They've seen us,' Adalon said and stood.

'They'll never take us,' Simangee said. Her face was drawn and Adalon could see scales under her eyes beginning to flake. She stood and lurched up the slope.

Targesh looked at Adalon. 'She isn't right.'

'I know. That evil cloud has touched her in some way.'

Targesh rumbled his displeasure. He took the reins of Simangee's riding beast and led it after her.

It was Simangee who now drove them higher.

Her face set, she pushed on. Adalon's spirit sank at her stumbling gait, but she refused his offers of assistance. Once, she nearly pitched headlong on a stretch of treacherous gravel. When Adalon sprang forward and took her arm, she would not look at him and her sigh sounded like a snarl.

A rocky ridge took them well up the slope of the mountain. Shadows began to creep over the rocky landscape to embrace them. Simangee laboured on, barely looking up to check their direction. Adalon and Targesh had difficulty keeping up, as a path had to be found for the riding beasts.

Eventually, after an hour's struggle, they were stopped by a deep fissure. It was a good stone's throw wide and extended as far as they could see across the mountain's flank. Smoke rose from it and Adalon wrinkled his snout at the sour, sulphurous smell.

Targesh looked at the fissure and then at the riding beasts. Adalon sighed. 'Let them go. They will manage without us.'

Silently, Adalon and Targesh divided their belongings between them. Simangee stood beside them, her gaze on the summit of Graaldon.

Targesh slapped each riding beast on the rump. They snorted and cantered off down the rocky slope. 'Good luck!' Adalon called after them. *They may have the best fate of the lot of us.*

Twelve

A deep, bone-shaking rumble came through the ground underfoot; smoke and flame spewed from the top of the mountain. Adalon gasped at the display, but was glad when the mountain settled quickly. Soon, a column of smoke was the only sign of life in the heights.

'The smoking mountain is unhappy,' Simangee said.

Targesh hefted the saddlebags and made sure his axe was secure. 'Bellyache.'

'Let's go and see,' Adalon suggested.

Simangee led them. She found a narrow path down the side of the chasm. Adalon marvelled at the way she picked out footholds where he could have sworn there was only smooth rock. When younger, he had been the climber of the three, bounding up and down trees using his spring, his claws and his tail for balance. But here Simangee climbed down as if she had lived in trees all her life.

When they reached the floor of the fissure, Adalon noticed that the rock beneath his feet was warm. Cracks vented smoke that singed his nostrils and made his eyes water. He coughed and scrambled, trying to keep Simangee in sight. He caught up to her just as she began climbing up the far face of the rocky cleft.

Adalon was torn. Should he follow Simangee, or wait for Targesh? Targesh was a poor climber at the best of times. His stocky frame was meant for the ground, not for the heights.

He looked up. Simangee had already disappeared through the smoke. He turned and waited.

He was glad. Targesh would never have made it to the top by himself. Adalon had to use all his climbing skill to find his way upwards, and he had to pause often to point out handholds and resting places to his burly friend.

Eventually, Adalon dragged himself over the lip of the fissure. He turned and hauled Targesh up.

Targesh nodded his thanks. 'Simangee?'

She stood waiting for them a short distance away. A ghost of a smile flitted across her face and, for a moment, the old Simangee was looking at them. Then she frowned. 'Let's go.'

Their way grew steeper and Adalon found that he was using his tail more and more to steady himself. Targesh clambered beside him, bent almost double, using his hands as much as his feet, not complaining, but definitely not comfortable. Simangee forged ahead without pausing.

Eventually, high above the plain, they edged around a massive rockfall and were confronted by a torrent of fire.

Molten rock was pouring from a large cave entrance. Red and orange and white flames leaped from it, and the whole side of the mountain glowed. It flowed down the slope for an arrow's flight or more before disappearing into the ground again. Adalon could feel the heat greedily licking at his face.

'The river of fire,' Simangee said. She rubbed her

face and winced as some scales fell away. 'This is our way into the Hidden Valley.'

Targesh frowned. 'How?'

Simangee shook her head impatiently and Adalon was pleased to see some of her normal spirit. 'Where the river of fire emerges from the mountainside there is an entrance to the Hidden Valley, so the book says. A path leads alongside the river of fire, a path the A'ak made, long ago.'

Adalon saw a rock fall into the river of fire. It flared and disappeared like a dry stick in a furnace. He squinted into the heat. 'You are sure about this?'

Simangee shivered and tore her gaze away from the blaze. 'Yes. It's the only way in. The Jarquin Ranges surround the valley, and they cannot be crossed.'

Targesh grunted and gestured back the way they had come. 'Wargrach?'

'He can't follow if we disappear before he sees us,' Adalon said.

A deep coughing roar came from where the river poured out of the mountainside. It was followed by a ball of flame and smoke that filled the cave mouth.

'Quickly, now,' Simangee said. 'Before the next outpouring.'

She set off. Adalon climbed after her. He was closest to the river of fire and he felt the heat through his thick traveller's cloak. Before too long he could smell singed fabric.

Targesh slipped and cursed. Adalon steadied himself, then dug his feet into thick ash. It kicked up and fell back, uncovering rusty metal.

Adalon swept the ash away with a hand and exposed a rusty spearhead. A long leaf shape, it had a strange twisted barb near the tip. 'I've never seen anything like this before.'

'From up there,' Targesh said, and gestured with one horn. 'The A'ak.'

Adalon looked up at the cave mouth. It was lit from within by orange light, and heat burst from it like water through a hole in a dam.

Simangee nodded. 'We must hurry. We don't have long.'

Adalon gritted his teeth and pushed on.

Thirteen

The cave mouth belched smoke and cascades of molten rock. Heat splashed on Adalon's face and he could also feel the heat in the rocks they were climbing over. He wished for gloves.

Wiping his face, coughing and spitting ash from his mouth, he turned to check the progress of their pursuers. The rock beneath his feet shifted and, as he caught his balance, something flashed into his vision. With Clawed One speed, he jerked back and an arrow shattered on the rock next to him. He peered through the smoke and orange light and saw figures clambering up the slope. 'They're almost upon us!' he cried. 'Targesh, to me! Sim, do you have any arrows left?'

Simangee seized his shoulder. She shook her head and jabbed a claw at the cave mouth. 'We must go! We have little time!'

Another arrow struck at his feet. He put a hand to the hilt of his sword, but Simangee refused to let him draw it.

He looked at her. She stared back with eyes that were rimmed with red. Was something lurking behind them? A shadow?

Targesh put a hand on Adalon's shoulder. 'Trust her.'

All was still for an instant, and in that time Adalon realised that trust was what bound all three of them together. If he couldn't trust Targesh and Simangee, who could he rely on? 'We are with you, Simangee,' he said.

Shouts and cries came from their pursuers. Adalon shepherded Simangee ahead of him. Targesh followed close behind.

Avoiding the river of molten rock that coursed from the cave mouth, Simangee scrambled over a fall of rubble at the entrance. Adalon went next, hissing at the hot rock beneath his hands. He held his tail high to stop it being burned. Inside the cave, a path by the side of the wall led them upwards, until they were looking down on the river of fire. He choked on the smoke and fumes, and, with tears in his eyes, looked around at the cave that stretched out in front of them.

Simangee hurried forward along the narrow, broken path. Adalon ran his hand against the smooth rock walls and realised that the cave had become a tunnel. The walls were almost glassy and reflected the red glow of the river of fire.

As they followed Simangee, Adalon felt the heat wrapping them up like a blanket. He felt it through the soles of his feet. A huge chuffing noise came from the river of fire to their left, echoing along the tunnel. Simangee looked back, wide-eyed, and waved them onwards.

Voices came from behind, hunting cries and screams rising over the noise. A roar of triumph went up, the grating, growling roar of a Toothed One, a roar that sounded down the ages from when the world was new. It made Adalon stop, stiffening in place. Small, he felt small, helpless and doomed. He was prey, and prey only existed to be eaten. He had no chance, no hope, nothing . . .

'Move,' Targesh grunted. He nudged Adalon with a horn, pricking his shoulder.

Adalon blinked and shook himself. He realised he'd experienced the power of a full-grown Toothed One. When he'd heard the roar, he'd frozen. If Targesh hadn't nudged him, he would have simply waited there to be killed.

Adalon whirled and shook his fist at General Wargrach and his troops. Jeers and cries went up. Anger seized Adalon. *I'm no soft-bellied, hairy-pelted, squeaking beast of prey!* he thought. Seething, he dragged his bow from his back and launched an arrow at them, then another, then another, until Targesh took his arm. 'It's no good. Follow Sim.'

Adalon took a deep breath and felt the anger leave him. It was foolish, standing here, trying to bring down Wargrach and his soldiers in this light. *Fight, fall back, fight again,* he recited to himself. *The Way of the Claw.*

Adalon jogged after Simangee. Targesh lumbered alongside, struggling in the heat. His great head and neck shield began to droop. Below the path, the river of fire widened into a bright orange-white lake. The path took them up, up until they were high on the wall of the tunnel, but still the heat was fierce. They stumbled to where Simangee was waiting. Adalon felt the breath searing in his throat. 'How much further?' he croaked.

Simangee pointed past the fiery lake. 'Look.'

Adalon held up a hand to shield himself from the red glow. He could see something. Because of the smoke he wasn't quite sure at first, but there it was . . . light! The healthy light of outdoors!

A fountain of molten rock burst from the lake. The three friends staggered back at the blast of heat. The plume of lava arced up until it struck the craggy ceiling overhead, where it splashed, sending red-hot globules of molten rock in all directions. Adalon ducked, but the nearest fell some distance away. He rose on his toe-claws and he wondered if the tunnel would collapse.

Simangee gestured ahead, then hurried on. Adalon and Targesh followed. With each step, the rock grew hotter. Adalon thought he could feel his skin starting to shrivel. His tail skimmed the rock and he hissed with pain.

'On,' grunted Targesh from behind him. 'Up.'

The path beside the lake of fire grew yet narrower.

Adalon looked down. The molten rock was alight with reds and oranges, with streamers of bright white that made his vision dance. The vast chuffing noise was even louder and he felt as if he were trapped in a giant bellows.

Heat beat at him and he saw that the lake was heaving. Great waves surged along the lake, along the river of fire, then down toward the cave entrance. Flame and smoke leaped high, licking the ceiling of the cave.

In a rush, they squeezed around a rocky spur and were past the lake. Light beckoned. Adalon broke into a run, yet couldn't catch Simangee. His heart felt as if it would burst as he scrambled up the slope, ignoring the pain in his hands and feet. The air began to grow thicker with smoke and he heard Targesh's throaty coughing from behind him.

Adalon looked up and peered ahead. He could dimly see Simangee, scrambling toward the light. He dug in his claws and dragged himself after her, trying not to choke on the smoke.

He looked up in time to see Simangee disappear. He surged forward and, suddenly, broke into open air.

In the dim twilight, Adalon cried out in relief and sucked in lungfuls of cool air. Then Targesh stumbled out of the tunnel and ran straight into him. They both rolled onto a mat of thick, green grass, Targesh's horns gouging long furrows as he fell face first.

Adalon sat up to see Simangee lying close to them. Her gaze was on the cave they had just left. 'The fiery lake is about to erupt. The cave will fill with molten rock before rolling out and down the mountainside. I think we got through just in time.'

'We did?' Targesh said. He glared at the cave mouth.

'Explorers were afraid to enter the tunnel until the A'ak discovered that the lake erupts regularly, allowing time to get through to the Hidden Valley.'

The mountain roared. Adalon clapped his hands to his ears as he was engulfed by the noise. It was like being pummelled by a thousand fists. He rolled onto his stomach and put his hands over his head. The ground shook. Smoke and heat burst from the cave – but no molten rock came their way.

Adalon lay there wondering when it would stop. *If* it would stop.

A few minutes later, all was still again.

Simangee sat and looked at the cave mouth. 'I don't think we have to worry about General Wargrach.'

Fourteen

Wargrach's head pounded with each step. He felt as if the top of his skull would fly off any minute. He staggered, fell, crawled, picked himself up and fell again, clenching his teeth to stop himself from screaming each time. Bright pain flared in his shoulder, his hip, the back of his head, his hands. His left arm hung at his side and he knew at least one of the bones was broken.

Wargrach turned his one good eye back to Graaldon, the smoking mountain. He snarled and tried to curse it, but the words caught in his scorched throat and sent him into a spasm of coughing. He bent double and the pain from his many burns and wounds blended together into one map of agony. This time, he did scream.

He was thankful that none of his troops had survived to hear him.

When the pain had receded, he opened his eye and stared at the velvet of the night sky. Stars looked down on him from between clouds stained orange from the glow of the fires of Graaldon.

The taste of defeat was sour in his mouth. In that accursed tunnel he had been close; his prey had almost been in his grasp. The youngling and his friends were nearly his.

At that moment, when the climax of the hunt was near, the blood had beat in his veins and he had known he was a true descendant of the Toothed Ones of old. The hunt, the chase with the promise of blood in the end. *That* was what he was meant for, that was what the greatest saur were meant for! Great saur dominate the weak, crush those who resist, destroy all enemies, rend them with tooth and claw.

Wargrach had surged ahead of his troops, leading them forward, an unstoppable force.

Then the tunnel erupted.

The sensation was vast, immense, a battering of sight, sound, feeling. Light and heat burst on them in an outrageous assault. Wargrach felt as if he had been slapped with a white-hot sheet of iron, then he was hurled through the air. He remembered touching rock and flame at the same time, seeing a shield slump and melt, hearing shrieks from the saur around him, smelling –

If it weren't for his secret cache of spells, he would have been lost. Blinded, he'd groped in the inner pocket of his jacket and seized the first bottle he touched. He flung it to the rocky floor and he was immediately surrounded by a protective cocoon. He knew it wouldn't last long, but for a moment the heat and noise were gone. Before he could do anything other than gasp for breath, however, a wave of molten rock picked up the cocoon. Wargrach was buffeted and rolled helplessly in the flood. Finally he was spat out of the tunnel onto the rocky slope. The cocoon dissolved and he was left staring at the cascade of lava belching from the tunnel mouth.

He rolled over, was sick, then swooned.

Later, lying on his bed of pain under the stars and clouds, trying to gather what little strength he had left, he finally managed to curse young Adalon of the Eastern Peaks.

The next morning, wet with ashy dew, Wargrach struggled to his feet and lurched away from the smoking mountain.

Once Adalon had peered inside the cave mouth and reassured himself that their pursuers were gone, they moved a short distance away to a grassy clearing. Targesh gathered some fallen wood from nearby scrubby plants and made a fire, and the three friends prepared a meal.

The moon was rising, huge and golden. By its light, Adalon was able to look out over the valley they had stumbled on. Adalon munched on dried meat he had in his pack. Despite being bruised and slightly toasted, he was amazed at what he saw. *Welcome to the Hidden Valley*, he thought.

The valley was entirely ringed by jagged mountains. They thrust up like sharp teeth and nowhere could Adalon see a gap in them. Graaldon was the largest of them. It rumbled and smoked constantly, but the wind took the smoke away from the valley, not toward it.

Adalon could see that the valley was narrow, barely a league from side to side. Thick woods started high up on the flanks of the mountains and spread down into the valley itself. He thought he could make out a river, snaking its way along the valley floor, and rocky outcrops pushing up through the forest.

It was on one of these outcrops, out in the middle of the valley, that the Lost Castle stood.

Even at this distance, and at night, Adalon could see that the Lost Castle was graceful. Its towers stood proudly, high above the valley floor. One was much taller than the other three and his gaze was drawn to it. He wondered who had lived there and what they had seen. Did they use it to study the heavens? Or was it a sentry tower to spy out enemies? He yearned to find out.

Adalon bit off another chunk of meat and chewed it thoughtfully. 'How far away is it, Simangee?'

Simangee looked up from the old book. The light of the campfire glittered in her eyes. 'I don't know.'

Adalon nodded, but continued to study his friend after she turned away.

She was still not herself, he was convinced of that. The encounter with the devil cloud had changed her.

'Further than it looks,' Targesh said. He was eating some tree fungus he had found while gathering firewood. He broke the great plates into pieces and ate them with delicate bites of his horned beak.

'A day's walking?' Adalon guessed.

'Yes, but we mustn't travel in the dark,' Simangee said. She shivered.

'Why not?'

'Traiths and screets haunt the valley at night, or so the book says. In the dark, the A'ak travelled in armed groups. It was safest. Otherwise, they stayed around a fire.'

Targesh snorted and thumped his tail on the ground. 'Need more wood.'

Simangee shrugged. 'We're safe near the cave. Traiths don't like the fumes, and screets have to stay near water.'

'Traiths? Screets? What are they?' Adalon asked. 'And what else does this book have to tell us?'

Simangee tilted the book to get more light. 'There is no description of traiths and screets. I think we're supposed to know what they are. Just like the black lurkers the book mentions.'

'Black lurkers?' Targesh grumbled. He looked at the trees around them with suspicion.

'This is not altogether a happy valley, then?' Adalon said.

'It was a refuge, a place of safety, especially once the Lost Castle was built. The beasts were a small price to pay.'

Adalon studied the far-off towers. 'Let us get there as soon as we can.'

Fifteen

The next morning, Adalon woke cold and stiff. He climbed out of his bedroll and while he stretched he looked out over the valley.

Under the blue sky, the vista looked different. Between the mountains it was like a green sea, so thick were the woods. A break in the trees showed that a river did indeed wind its way through the centre of the valley.

The Lost Castle stood in the middle of it all, grey stone built on grey stone.

'Beautiful,' Targesh said, nodding a horn in the direction of the castle. He was sitting with his cloak wrapped around him. He had agreed to take the last watch for the night. Adalon guessed he regretted it.

'A quiet night?' he asked as his friend stood and stretched, tilting his neck shield from side to side. He stamped his feet and thumped his tail on the ground.

'No traiths, screets, black lurkers.'

'You kept the fire going well.'

Targesh snorted and ignored him.

Simangee rolled over. 'Is it morning?'

Adalon studied her face. She looked exhausted. 'Yes.'

'We should go.'

Despite his concern, Adalon agreed. He itched to be off; he was eager to be moving again, especially with a destination in sight.

It was midmorning when they reached the river.

'Fresh,' Adalon said. He crouched and scooped up a handful of water. 'Cold, too, straight from the mountains.'

Targesh stood well back from the river, as if he were worried it was about to reach out and carry him away. Simangee leaned listlessly against a tree, her head drooping.

Adalon stood on the bank. From the size of the river, he doubted if the valley lacked for water, even in full summer. He could see ducks, cranes and darters happily at home on the river; fish would be plentiful.

He looked around and saw that Simangee wasn't looking at the river life. She was scraping at a tangle of creeper with a toe-claw.

'What have you found?' Adalon asked as he joined her.

'A road.' Simangee knelt and dragged the creeper aside. She revealed flat, well-worked stone. As more creeper was torn away, more stone showed through. 'It leads to the castle.'

'Your book reveals this, too?'

Simangee stood. 'The road follows the river. If we keep to it we should find the travelling easier.'

Adalon was cheerful as he walked next to the road. The valley was a pleasant place and it felt good to have grass underfoot after the leagues of rock they had trudged through.

The forest was rich with oak and beech. Game fled from their approach in numbers that meant the cooking pot would never be empty. *Many saur could live here*, Adalon thought as a pair of rabbits scampered over a knoll and disappeared. *Hundreds*.

It could be a pleasant enough place, he decided. A place to settle, to stay, far away from the troubles of the world.

He sighed. *I can't forget my vow*, he thought.

It troubled him. As he walked, he wondered if he was driven to save Thraag, or to avenge his father. The two blurred. Doing one would achieve the other, but was it right? Were his noble aims just a pretence to cover his rage? He shook his head and wished for simpler times.

Every half a league or so, the road brought them to a clearing, at each of which they found the remains of an old farm. At the first of these, they explored the fallen-down farmhouse and outbuildings, trying to find a clue about those who had lived there. Adalon's puzzlement grew, however, as they found little left behind. No clothes, no personal belongings, only dishes and pots and farm tools.

Each farm did have a small reward for them. Orchards seemed to have been important, and the three friends found apples, almonds, pears and even some late peaches. They were all grateful for the addition to their diet. Even Adalon, a meat-eater, enjoyed fruit.

Along the roadside they came across small, ruined forts. Adalon approved of the way the A'ak had sited these forts at regular distances. *Good planning*, he thought, and decided it was the sort of planning that was common sense to military people.

His curiosity about the A'ak was growing.

Sixteen

After some hours' marching, evening began to draw in. The shadows of the mountains and the trees crept across the valley. Adalon and Targesh were alert, watching both sides of the road and keeping Simangee between them.

Adalon clicked his claws together nervously, alive to every sound. Targesh carried his axe and stumped along holding it ready.

The road took them on a wide curve and the river disappeared behind a wall of head-high bushes. Then the growth cleared and they could see the river again.

All three stood and stared.

There, on an island in the middle of the river, stood the Lost Castle.

Adalon glanced at Targesh. He was eyeing the water with distaste. 'You go,' Targesh said. 'I'll stay here.'

Adalon knew that getting Targesh over to the Lost Castle would be a trial. Targesh mistrusted boats, never swam, and felt that those who went to sea were mad. He was of the firm view that water was for drinking and, occasionally, bathing.

Targesh took a step back from the bank, then another. He crossed his arms and glared at the river as if it were an old enemy just waiting for its chance to drown him.

Adalon looked up the riverbank and saw crumbled stone pilings that led across the river toward the island. Moss turned the stonework into a patchwork of grey and green. A bird landed in a nest on top of one piling. It had a small fish in its beak. 'There was a bridge here, once,' said Adalon.

Targesh grunted. Bridges were acceptable. Barely.

'It's a ruin. Not much use now,' Simangee said. She sank to the ground, her chin resting on her chest and her tail curled around her knees.

Adalon looked across the river then up at the sky. The sun was getting low. With night coming on, he was mindful of the traiths and screets. He looked at the trees nearby. Perhaps they could fell a few and lay them over the remains of the bridge —

Something in the trees caught his gaze. He walked over and his eyes widened when he saw, hanging from a branch, a small golden pipe.

Even though the silken cord on which it hung was frayed and weatherworn, the pipe shone as brightly as the noonday sun. Adalon reached out and seized it. The cord snapped and he felt the warm tingle that meant magic.

He hissed. *Whatever happened to looking first, then acting?*

Adalon held the pipe in the palm of his hand and poked at it with a claw. It was as long as his hand and light as a feather. It had a mouthpiece and no fingerholes. It thrummed with magic.

What was going to be the cost of this magic?

He felt the pipe quiver. Immediately, he held it at arm's length and bared his teeth. His tail twitched uneasily.

The pipe trembled more strongly. Adalon could

feel its magic as a throbbing, deep in the bones of his hand and arm. His scales prickled as if he were in a sandstorm.

Fear curled around Adalon's heart like a black snake. It was the fear of the unknown, the fear that leaps up at an unexpected noise in the dark. It was the fear that makes the young close their eyes and hope that it – whatever it is – can't see them. It was the fear that comes from imagination – thinking the worst that *might* happen and the worst that *could* happen and then building it up until it becomes the dizzy heights of terror.

Simangee turned from the river and looked at Adalon. 'What is in your hand?'

Adalon held up his find. 'I don't know.'

Simangee lifted her head. 'I can feel its magic from here!' She peered at it. 'A pipe! Play it! Or give it to me!'

Adalon grimaced. Simangee was apt to fiddle with magic, unworried by the consequences. She did not understand Adalon's caution where magic was concerned.

He couldn't allow her to use the pipe. Exhausted as she was, still suffering from the touch of the evil cloud, toying with more magic would go hard with her.

I do not want to do this, Adalon thought as he raised the pipe to his mouth. He paused. Targesh looked at him with concern, but his attention was caught by Simangee. She was looking at him with an expression that was a mixture of greed, sorrow and understanding.

A thin wailing came from a distance. Simangee shuddered. 'Screets.'

That was enough. Adalon took a deep breath and blew on the golden pipe.

The whole valley seemed to echo with the sound. Birds sprang into the air and trees bent as if struck by a mighty wind. The voice of the pipe was as strong and golden as the sound of a mighty war horn. It spoke of battle and glory and triumph, but underneath, the music was haunted with grief and loss.

For an instant, Adalon had a vision of a battle led by golden, indistinct figures he knew were the A'ak. They rode in cruel splendour, cutting a swathe through a force made up of misshapen Toothed Ones, Plated Ones, Horned Ones and Clawed Ones.

But while he saw this, Adalon was aware of a ghostly scene underlying this vision of triumph. It was the battlefield the next day, after the charge of the A'ak. It was strewn with dead and dying saur. Carrion birds hopped over corpses at their leisure. Flies were thick in the air.

The double scene disappeared. Pain flared in the bones of his hand. Like the river of fire under Graaldon, it ran up his arm and spread through his whole body in an instant.

Adalon stiffened. Waves of agony coursed through his body. He felt as if he were about to erupt. He tried to let go of the pipe, but his hand refused.

His vision turned pink, then began to deepen toward red. It was as if he were looking at Targesh and Simangee through crimson silk.

Through the torture, Adalon tried to fling the pipe away, but his fist remained clenched around it.

'Adalon,' Targesh said. 'What's wrong?'

Adalon could not speak. All he could do was suffer.

With all his might, he strove to let go of the pipe, but he could not. Then, distantly, like the sound of a far-off bell, one of the most puzzling lessons in the Way of Claw came to him.

When you can hold a moment in the claws of one hand, not allowing it to move, then you have achieved the true Way of the Claw.

He had often asked his father about it, but Ollamon had simply shaken his head. 'When you are ready, all will be clear,' was his only response.

Adalon could feel himself weakening. He ground his teeth together and felt blood in his mouth. He knew he had to let go of the pipe or he would perish.

Remember the Claw, he told himself. *Hold the moment.*

Adalon banished everything from his mind, apart from the pipe in his hand. Gradually, the pain faded, then vanished – but he barely noticed it had gone. He couldn't see Targesh, nor Simangee, nor the trees, river and castle beyond. All he could see was his clenched fist.

The entire world paused, and Adalon held on to the moment. Time stretched. In between one heartbeat and the next was an eternity. In this eternity he realised that the pain had not disappeared; he had simply put it aside and looked past it. Without the distraction of the pain, he was able to gather himself. He pondered the muscles in his hands, the tendons, the bones. *Open*, he ordered, and his fist unclenched.

The magic pipe fell to the ground and the moment fled. The world rushed in and he staggered, assaulted by the sounds, smells and sensations that he had been apart from for a long, long, instant. He took a step back and hissed. He stared at the pipe on the ground, his heart hammering.

Targesh's mouth hung open and he stared at the pipe as well. 'Adalon?'

'Look!' Simangee said. 'The river!'

Adalon, fresh from one wonder, was confronted with another. From the riverbank to the Lost Castle, the river had stopped flowing. It was smooth and still, as if a long pane of glass had been laid across it.

Simangee stood and reached out a foot. 'It's hard.' She took a step, and another.

'You're standing on water,' Adalon said, stunned.

'Magic,' Simangee called as she stood there, arms outstretched. 'Hurry, it may not last.'

Magic, Adalon thought. He flexed his hand. *And pain was the price.*

After an instant's hesitation, Adalon scooped up the pipe and dropped it into a pocket. He then seized his pack and hurried to the riverbank. One deep breath and he stepped out to join his Crested One friend.

The river was solid and dry underfoot, but Adalon could clearly see the stones of the riverbed beneath. A fish swam by, not worried at all by the strange creatures walking just over its head.

Adalon looked back to the riverbank. Targesh stood there, shifting uneasily, staring down at the water.

'Come, Targesh. It's safe,' Adalon called.

Targesh looked up. 'Water? Safe? Hah!'

Adalon strode back to his friend. 'Close your eyes. I'll lead you across.'

Targesh looked at Adalon, searching his face. He nodded and held out his arm.

'Right,' Adalon said. 'On the count of three. One, two, *three*!'

Targesh grunted as they took the first step. Adalon glanced at him and saw that his friend's eyes were screwed shut. For a moment he thought it was comical, the way the huge Horned One was afraid of water, but then he shrugged. *We all have our fears*, he thought. Together, they marched to where Simangee waited in the middle of the river.

Simangee was the first to reach the island. She stumbled onto the shore, followed by Adalon. Targesh lurched, opened his eyes, then took a few more steps before turning around and glaring at the river.

'We're safe,' Simangee said. 'The river is flowing again.'

Adalon turned to see that the river had lost its hardness. The current had returned, and ripples played on the river's surface in the last, dying light of the sun.

He stared. Emerging from the scrub on the bank was a long, black shape. Four-legged and furred, with the sinuous grace of a hunter, it threw back its head and gave a high-pitched, choking wail. It sounded frustrated, disappointed, hungry.

'None too soon,' Adalon said, and patted the pocket that held the magic pipe.

'Traith, screet or black lurker?' Simangee said,

staring at the creature. It was long and low, but at that moment it reared up on its hind legs, sniffing the air. It was as tall as two full-grown Toothed Ones.

'Does it matter?' Targesh said.

The black creature dropped to all fours and flowed back through the undergrowth.

Simangee shivered. 'I'm glad it's there and we're here.'

Seventeen

Adalon woke with the sun in his eyes. Groaning, he held up a hand and peered through his claws.

He had fallen asleep in a room in the Lost Castle. It had taken three flights of stairs to get to it, but there were many storeys above. It had appealed to Adalon because of its high ceilings and two large windows, which opened out onto balconies with fine views of the courtyard and the river beyond the walls.

The room contained little furniture, and this also attracted Adalon. It made him uneasy to think of using a bed where the last dreams were dreamed hundreds of years ago. Instead, he arranged his travel-worn bedroll in a corner.

Simangee stood on one of the balconies. The stonework around her was carved with the likenesses of birds and fish. Behind her lay the valley.

She was singing.

Smiling, Adalon got to his feet. He winced when he realised he'd slept awkwardly on his tail. He stretched for a moment, enjoying his friend's music. It was a mixture of trills and rolls, a happy, rollicking tune that made the day sparkle.

'You're feeling better,' he said.

She stopped singing and turned to him. 'Much.'

Adalon studied her. The dullness had gone from the scales under her eyes. She looked rested and refreshed, full of energy. He stared into her eyes, looking for the shadow that had haunted her. She looked back at him, grinning, eyes bright, except for – no, he was mistaken. Simangee was herself again.

'I see nothing there,' he announced.

'I beg your pardon?' Simangee said. 'Am I nothing? What about this, then?'

She reached out with her claws and nipped him on the hand.

'Tcha!' he said, clicking his tongue. 'What was that for?'

'To show you I'm not nothing.'

Adalon laughed. It was good to have his friend back. 'The evil cloud? You're rid of it?'

Simangee immediately looked more sombre. 'I hope so.' She shuddered. 'It was horrible. I felt as if I was walking in darkness.' She glanced at him. 'It was a creature of the A'ak, you know. A magical servant. They used it to control those who needed controlling.'

'I didn't know what to do. I thought getting you to safety was the best thing.'

Simangee patted him on the shoulder. 'It was. It gave me time to draw on the Way of the Crest. I was able to use the music of the world to counter the cloud's taint.'

The Ways of the other saur were a mystery to Adalon. He knew of them, of course, and always listened respectfully whenever Targesh or Simangee spoke of their beliefs, but they were as foreign to him as another language.

'The music of the world?' he said.

Simangee glanced at Adalon and seemed to weigh up how much to tell him. 'The Way of the Crest is based on the fact that the entire world is one great, musical composition. Everything has its part, everything contributes to the harmony that binds the world together. Part of our duty when we study the Way of the Crest is to try to hear the music of the world, to try to respond to it.' She shook her head. 'I'm still young, still learning. In the past, I've tried my best, but the music of the world has eluded me. Until last night.'

'You heard it?'

'I did. I was concentrating, aware of the taint of the evil cloud within me. I wanted to banish it completely and I knew that the Way of the Crest was my only hope. I remembered its lessons, its music; I studied each melody, watched every note.' Simangee paused, her gaze distant, her face thoughtful. 'Then, for one brief moment, I sensed the music of the world.' She looked at her friend. 'It was majestic, Adalon. Vast, swelling and mighty – but it was almost too much. I took what I could, found the part that helped me most, and then it faded away. I was left with a small fragment, a melody that I used to rid myself of the last trace of the evil cloud.'

Adalon studied his friend. Her face was merry and she snorted.

'Stop looking at me like that, Adalon. I'm perfectly well!'

'Of course.'

At that moment, Targesh clumped into the room. 'Big place.' He stopped and sneezed.

'What have you found?' Adalon asked.

Targesh shrugged. 'Lots of dust.'

'What else?'

'Empty rooms. No food, though.'

'Any sign of the A'ak?' Simangee asked, and a shadow crossed her face.

'Nothing.'

'The A'ak left things behind,' Simangee said slowly, frowning. 'Or so the book says.'

'Helpful things?' Adalon asked.

'Weapons. Magical items.'

'Food?' Targesh asked.

'Not unless it's magical food. And I don't think you'd like what it would do to you.'

Targesh grunted. 'Plenty of greenery out there. That'll do.'

'Look for some berries and nuts,' Simangee said. 'There could be fruit trees somewhere nearby, too.'

Targesh tilted his head. 'Adalon?'

'We're beside a river. I can live on fish.'

'Good,' Targesh said. 'I'll get something for Simangee and me.'

'She and I will explore the castle,' Adalon said, and looked at his friends. 'Thanks to Simangee, we are safe from the Queen's rage.' He put a hand on her shoulder. 'Without your cleverness, we would never have found this place.'

Simangee squirmed and smiled. 'Thank Targesh, too. It was his doing that got you out of the dungeon.'

'Of course.' He turned to Targesh. 'You are our strength, my friend. I thank you.'

Targesh rumbled happily.

'But this is just the start of our journey,' Adalon said. 'Now we must do what we can to stop the Queen's mad plans to conquer Krangor.'

'The three of us against Thraag?' Simangee said.

Adalon shook his head. 'Not against Thraag. Against Tayesha.'

Simangee looked downcast. 'We are so few.'

'We are all we have. We will do what we can and it will be a beginning.'

The Lost Castle was silent and dim. The air was heavy with the weight of centuries. Adalon felt like an intruder as Simangee and he moved through halls, ballrooms, galleries and chambers of unknown purpose. The castle did not seem to resent their presence; Adalon thought it was distant, aloof, patient. It had survived long after the A'ak had disappeared, and he wondered if it would simply go on forever, occupying this place, outlasting the years.

Adalon admired the cleverness of the builders. They had a way of working with stone and wood so that everything fitted together seamlessly, as if the blocks and beams had simply grown there. He examined joints and was impressed at how they had been made without nails, almost as if the timbers had been encouraged to bind themselves together.

'How long has it been since this place was abandoned?' he asked Simangee as they entered a huge open area. Stone pillars held up a vast, domed ceiling. They were carved in the likeness of tree trunks, with rough bark and patches of moss.

'Long before the seven kingdoms were founded,' Simangee whispered. Dust lay thick on the floor, in places higher than their ankles.

They moved on.

The furniture the A'ak had left behind had survived the years. Many of the wall-hangings and drapes were still bright and colourful. Adalon was intrigued by a particularly intricate tapestry filling one entire wall of a long narrow room.

He gazed at the tapestry and then looked around the room, wondering about its purpose. Rows of seats lined the long walls, leaving an empty aisle in the middle. Light poured through windows high in the walls. The columns supporting the ceiling were sheathed in gold and glittered in the sunlight.

Adalon stood still, admiring the tapestry. It was a scene in this same hall, but the hall was full. Rank on rank of richly dressed nobles, scholars and soldiers were listening to a tall figure. They were a mixture of saur – Long-necked Ones, Toothed Ones, Clawed Ones, Plated Ones and others. The figure standing on the dais was wrapped in cloud and barely an outline could be seen. The image disturbed Adalon in a way that he couldn't quite put his claw on.

'There,' Simangee said, interrupting his thoughts. 'She stood there.'

She was pointing to the dais under the tapestry.

On the dais was a simple wooden chair. 'That was her throne.'

'Who?'

'The Queen of the A'ak.'

Together, they walked up the long aisle. When they reached the dais, Adalon studied the wooden chair. 'A simple throne.'

'This hall was where she ruled this kingdom, where the A'ak made their decisions.'

'But where are they? Where did they go?'

'Mysteries,' Simangee said, and she stared at the tapestry. 'We are left with mysteries.'

Eighteen

Room by room, Adalon and Simangee explored. The outside world had not entered the castle, even in rooms where the shutters had been left open, exposing them to the elements. No birds had built nests, no leaves had been blown in. All was quiet and solemn. The dust was the only sign that the castle had not been built yesterday.

Ballrooms and kitchens, studies and workshops, banquet halls and libraries full of books in the indecipherable A'ak script – all looked as if the A'ak had simply stepped out for a while. It put Adalon on edge, and he itched for answers.

What if they decide to come back? he thought,

then chased the thought away as foolish.

Adalon was pleased when he found the armoury near the gatehouse, just inside the walls. The smell of oiled metal and rope reminded him of the hours Targesh and he had spent in the armoury at High Battilon. He took a halberd from a rack. 'There are enough weapons to fit out an army,' he said to Simangee.

'Of course.'

The stone walls were lined with racks full of swords, pikes, partisans, maces and dozens of weapons Adalon did not recognise. Chain mail hung on wooden dummies. Stacks of helmets stood against walls. A door led to a workshop where a cold furnace stood. Adalon could see, in his mind's eye, a blacksmith hammering metal, with youngsters pumping the bellows and quenching red-hot metal.

A large iron cabinet stood against one wall of the armoury, twice as wide as Adalon's armspan. Typical of A'ak design, its dull, black surface was etched with ornamentation – swirls and wreaths, vines and fruit, flowers and branches with leaves. Adalon ran a claw over intertwined stars and vegetation, then shivered and drew back.

'Magic.' He wiped his hands together in distaste.

Simangee came to his side. 'You feel magic, but I can see it.'

'You can see magic?'

'Ever since that cloud touched me, especially when it's strong magic.' She rubbed her eyes. 'It's a haze on a hot day, or oil on water, something like that,' she finished lamely. 'I saw it on the pipe you found. And now this.'

Adalon patted his pocket and felt the pipe still there. 'Is the cabinet's magic evil or good?'

'Magic is neither evil nor good. It is simply a tool, like a hammer or a saw.'

'A hammer can be used for bad purposes, as well as good.'

'Yes.'

Adalon frowned at the magical cabinet. 'I wonder what's inside.'

Simangee laughed. 'We're in an armoury, Adalon. What would you expect to find in a cabinet in an armoury?'

'Weapons. And in a magical cabinet I would expect to find magical arms.' He looked at Simangee. 'How do we open it?'

'It has a keyhole.'

Adalon peered at the slot surrounded by an intricate spiral of leaves and diamonds. 'And where is the key?'

'Somewhere safe, I imagine.'

Targesh appeared in the doorway. 'Found something. Come and see.'

Adalon put a hand on the cabinet and felt the ripple of magic again. Something important was in there, he was sure.

Simangee trotted to Targesh, her eyes bright, her tail swaying. 'Which way?'

Adalon sighed and followed, promising to come back to the mysterious cabinet.

Targesh wouldn't respond to Simangee's excited questions about what he had found. He led them through a large, wood-panelled hall, into a corridor. After lighting a lantern he ushered them along the stone-lined corridor, where each block was carved with geometric patterns that made Adalon's head spin.

'There.' Targesh pointed toward the end of the corridor.

Simangee gave an excited trill through her crest. 'An iron wall! What's it here for?'

Targesh led them closer. 'No,' Adalon said, 'it's not a wall. It's a pair of doors.'

The two doors met in the middle, and on the right-hand side of where they met were seven locks. Each lock was as big as Adalon's head, bright silver against the midnight-black metal of the door itself. The key slots were all different. Adalon scratched his chin with a thumb-claw and tried to imagine what sort of keys would be required to open such locks.

The top lock, above Adalon's head, had a key slot in the shape of an irregular pentagon, ridged and knurled. The others were equally strange: curved, twisted, branching. The bottom one looked like three concentric circles and Adalon couldn't see how it would work.

Simangee stood with her hands on her hips. 'Well, this tells us something.'

'It does?' Targesh said.

'Whatever is inside must be valuable. They wouldn't have gone to all this trouble, otherwise.'

Adalon nodded. 'This could be the main strong-room for the castle.'

Targesh pounded on the metal. It boomed dully. 'Thick.'

'And it has magic about it, too,' Simangee said.

Adalon took half a step backward before he realised what he was doing. Sheepishly, he tried to pretend he was getting a better view of the doors. He stroked his chin. 'Well, we're not going to get in without the keys, are we Sim?'

'Let me think about this.' She smiled a little and turned to face the doors. 'Call it a challenge.'

Adalon settled himself to wait, crossing his arms on his chest. He knew that patience was a good thing to practise, to balance his Clawed One impulsiveness, so he was almost disappointed when Simangee spun around, beaming.

'You have something?' Adalon asked.

'Perhaps. I might have a way to open this thing.' She tapped the door with her tail.

'You know where the keys are?' Targesh asked.

'Not exactly.' She grinned. 'Remember: the A'ak were the masters of deception and cunning. What if they could make the door safe by guile instead of brute strength?' She hummed a little. 'I think the seven locks are just a distraction.'

'How do we open it, then?' Adalon asked.

Simangee was enjoying herself. 'Let's consider

another cunning A'ak device: the secret passage across the river.'

'The golden pipe,' Adalon said. 'It summoned the magic.'

Simangee put a claw on her cheek. 'Hmm. Sometimes I think you were meant to find that pipe.' She waved that thought away before Adalon could pursue it. 'We don't have find any magical musical instruments around here, but I wonder if the A'ak did use one here, all those years ago.'

'So we need to find another magical pipe instead of a set of magical keys? I don't see that we're any better off.'

'No?' Simangee said. 'I might be able to use my musical skills and my knowledge of magic, to try to find the sound that will open the door.'

'Good idea,' Targesh said. 'You can do it.'

Simangee waved Adalon and Targesh back from the door. She stood with her palms touching the metal surface and her head turned to one side. 'This way,' she explained, 'I'll be able to hear and feel what's happening.'

Simangee took a deep breath, then lifted her chin and sang.

Adalon had always admired his friend's musical ability. She could turn her hand to any instrument and make tunes to set a party dancing, or she could sing a song of mourning which would leave every eye moist. Her music had the power to move souls.

Adalon listened in awe as Simangee sang to the iron doors, trying to coax them open. She sang wordless tunes that soared and dipped. When the doors quivered, she repeated a particular musical phrase, then again, but when it had no further effect she turned the phrase around, then added to it, then she returned to the original, singing it more slowly, then faster and faster until it was a shrill whine.

Simangee stopped, dropping her arms to her sides and panting. 'I nearly had it,' she said, her face downcast. 'It was as if they *wanted* to open, but I couldn't find the next notes to shift them any further.'

Adalon reached into the pocket of his tunic and took out the golden pipe. 'What if you heard this again? Could it help you?'

Simangee brightened. 'It might. If I could listen to it and feel its magic, it might point the way.'

Adalon looked at the pipe and realised that he was holding it in his claws, as if it were hot. His mouth was dry; he was afraid of it.

I will not let such a thing conquer me, he thought. He put it to his mouth and blew.

This time, as the pure sound of the pipe echoed from the walls, Adalon felt as if he were freezing to death. His bones ached with cold and his whole body was seized with violent shivering. Iciness wrapped around him, so chill it burned.

He felt Targesh's arm on his shoulders. 'What's wrong?'

Then, a sound rose, pure and clear, and the cold vanished. He shook himself and saw Simangee standing in front of the iron doors, arms spread, head back, eyes closed as she embraced the music. From her throat, and resonating through her crest, came an outpouring, a run of notes that climbed, descended, then – just as it seemed they would go on forever – ended.

The iron doors swung back without a sound.

Nineteen

Adalon gasped at what was revealed. Carefully, as if it were a dream where he might wake at any minute, he stepped through the doorway with Simangee and Targesh at his back.

The strongroom was as large as a ballroom. It was full, overflowing, *bursting* with treasure.

Shelves and racks lined the walls, full of crystal vases, golden ornaments and statues carved out of whole rubies and sapphires. Ropes of pearls hung from hooks. Large chests sat on the floor, all open, and all full of gold coins. Piles of golden trinkets reached up to the ceiling. Sacks of gems spilled over silver plates. Shimmering cloth in rolls the height of a tall saur stood like sentinels among crates of silver bars. Jewel-encrusted drinking horns, tankards and ornamented doublets hung from hooks.

Adalon clenched his fists together and bared his teeth. He could see the fulfilment of his vow in this very room. With this fortune he could *buy* an army that would stop Queen Tayesha.

He could imagine it. The finest soldiers, with equipment that would make his enemy tremble, then throw down their arms and run away. Cavalry, archers, foot soldiers, the best money could buy. They would come from all over Krangor to fight for him. He would lead them, a host to sweep Queen Tayesha from power.

Adalon saw that avenging his father and helping the saur of the world could both be achieved with the wealth around him. It made him light-headed and he settled himself, sobering.

Such good fortune was unlooked for, and the reputation of the A'ak made him uneasy. Wealth could be a trap for the unwary. He promised himself that he would be alert for danger. But, he argued, it would be foolish to ignore such usefulness.

He wandered among the riches. Numbly, he saw

Simangee and Targesh picking up one delicate object after another, wonder on their faces. Targesh looped precious necklaces around his horns. Simangee stood, draped in cloth of gold, hands on hips, laughing at him.

Brooches and bracelets. Crowns and rings. Orbs, pendants, necklaces of intricate beauty, baubles, curios, works of art. There was so much that Adalon began to feel overpowered by the opulence about him.

He turned, surveying the room, feeling dizzy. He saw a kingdom's worth of emeralds in a trunk. On the shelf above it stood a chess set with pieces carved from diamonds and black pearls. His heart ached at the sight of an exquisite robin made of spun silver.

Toward the back of the room, the riches were carelessly displayed. Bags of coins had split and spilled. A set of silver serving platters, each as large as a wheel, were roughly stacked against a wall. Golden cutlery was heaped willy-nilly in boxes. Adalon wondered if the keepers of the treasure had become bored with such wonders.

As he was about to leave, he saw something out of place. Near the door, in a niche in the wall at head height, was a key ring with three plain keys. In a room full of precious metals and gems, these ordinary items stood out like coal in the snow.

Adalon took the key ring in his hand, then nearly dropped it. *Magic*! he thought as he felt the familiar thrumming. He held the keys gingerly in his claws: one black iron, one dull brass, one made of hard, dark wood.

Simangee joined him and looked over his shoulder. 'I can see their magic.'

At that moment, Targesh gave a shout that echoed around the treasure chamber. 'Riding beasts!'

Adalon and Simangee looked at each other and burst out laughing. 'Where are you, Targesh?' Adalon called.

'Here!'

They found him at the far end of the chamber, behind a tall lacquer screen with scenes of the Hidden Valley on it. He was standing in front of three brass statues of riding beasts.

Two of the steeds were life-sized, slender beasts that looked as if they could outrun the wind. The other steed was heavier, a war charger with strength in its back and flanks. Adalon walked around them and marvelled at their exquisitely moulded manes and tails. Their hoofs, their flanks, their ears – all glowed the bright yellow-gold of brass. Saddles were cast into their backs and supple, braided brass reins and stirrups hung in place.

'Fine statues, Targesh,' Adalon said. 'But hardly worth keeping with the other treasures here.'

'They're magic,' Simangee said.

Targesh frowned at Simangee. 'She sees magic, Targesh,' Adalon explained. 'These keys are magical, too.'

'A brass key. For brass riding beasts?' Targesh suggested.

Adalon looked at Simangee. She nodded slowly. 'They belong together.'

Targesh pointed to a keyhole in the muzzle of the nearest riding beast.

Adalon took a deep breath. The steed stared at him with metal eyes, strange and distant. He wondered what those eyes had seen.

He raised the brass key, fitted it into the slot and turned it. He stood back.

With the sound of metal shifting on metal, the riding beast swivelled its head. Then it lowered its neck and gazed directly at Adalon. One hoof pawed at the ground and the stone rang. For a moment, it stood still, then its entire body quivered, making the sound of a thousand tiny cymbals.

Adalon reached out and touched the brass beast on the muzzle. Its snort was like a bell.

'It likes you,' Targesh said, grinning.

'I hope so.' Adalon took the reins in one hand and stood by the steed's flank. He patted its neck. The beast boomed like a kettledrum.

'Hollow,' Targesh said.

'I'd be hollow, too,' Simangee said, 'after so long alone.'

Adalon slid his foot in the stirrup and heaved himself into the saddle.

The riding beast shifted its weight, metal sliding on metal as it adjusted its balance. The saddle was cold and hard and Adalon made a note to use a blanket next time. He flicked the reins and clicked his tongue. 'Forward, oh riding beast.'

Targesh and Simangee moved to either side as the brass riding beast walked forward, lifting its hoofs high over the field of treasure.

Twenty

'A stripling, Wargrach, a mere youth! I set you to find and punish him and this is how you return!'

Anger warred with pain inside Wargrach. He bit down on both. 'He is dead, Your Majesty. I survived, but he perished in the fire that came from the mountain.' His voice, once deep and powerful, now whistled and bubbled through a ruined mouth. His jaw ached with the effort of shaping the words, but he'd learned to ignore it. He had learned much in his long ordeal, dragging himself from the feet of Graaldon back to Challish.

He leaned on his staff, lifted his head and peered

at Queen Tayesha with his one good eye. She stood with her back to the window of the Morning Room, outlined against the greenery. Late afternoon light surrounded her. It hurt Wargrach's eye to look and he turned away.

'You survived, Wargrach? It may have been better if you had not. What use are you now?'

Wargrach longed to rest on his tail, but it was still healing. The physicians said it was never going to support him again, but he knew better. 'Your Majesty, I am your servant. I will join the Bondorborar campaign.'

Queen Tayesha appeared in front of him. With a claw under his chin, she lifted his massive head. His wounds screamed, but he did not make a sound.

The Queen looked him in the eye. 'Oh yes, Wargrach. You are certainly my servant. You must never forget that.'

She took her claw away and his head sagged. Wargrach stifled a hiss of pain.

'Wargrach,' she continued, 'you are no good in the capital any more, so I have a small task that will take you far away. You may yet be of some small assistance.'

Wargrach gripped his staff until his claws bit into the wood. He wanted to turn on the Queen, slash at her, strike her down, show her that even though he was maimed he still followed the Way of the Tooth: *Mock not the warrior in his time of torment.*

He stilled his fury, knowing better than to give in to it. She could kill him before he laid a claw on her, such were her enchantments. No. It was better to endure her, then retire and make his plans.

'Tell me, Your Majesty.'

'Leave now for Sleeto. Take twenty troops and establish a base. Five hundred will soon be on their way to you. I want that fortress built on the border with Callibeen. No work has been done on it for months. The local lord has not cooperated as he should have.'

'Sleeto, Your Majesty?'

'Immediately.'

Wargrach felt as if he had fallen in mud but found a gold coin in it. Being sent to the Eastern Peaks was no punishment, not when he still wielded power in the region. Sleeto would do very nicely, very nicely indeed.

'Thank you, Your Majesty.'

'Leave now, through the garden gate. I don't want you limping through the palace.'

Queen Tayesha stared at her once-proud general as he retreated through the cycads and ginkgo trees of the garden. Evening was settling, and the shadows looked as if they were reaching out to embrace him.

Who would she confide in now? Wargrach had been the only one who had understood her dreams for Thraag and for all of Krangor. She knew he had treachery in his heart but, being aware of this, she felt she had Wargrach's measure.

She had planned to use him to further her ends, then discard him. Queen Tayesha straightened. Great sacrifices must be made, for the good of all.

She turned away from the window and walked to the small writing desk she had had brought to the Morning Room. She unlocked the drawer, quelled a guardian spell she had placed on it, and removed her journal.

A careful worker does not discard a useful tool, she wrote, *even when it has been badly damaged.*

Rather, the worker turns the tool to other uses – ones for which it is still fit.

Of course, the worker then obtains newer, better tools to replace the old.

Twenty-one

The day after they had found the treasury, Adalon watched from a balcony as Targesh wobbled on the giant brass riding beast. The Horned One was grinning like a tot with a new toy.

It had been Simangee who suggested that Targesh try mounting the largest of the three brass beasts. Targesh was often slow to come to new things and Adalon had been surprised when he agreed.

After a few hours, Targesh had managed to trot the riding beast around the courtyard. Adalon noted how the steed shifted underneath Targesh's uncertain seat, ensuring he never fell.

'Adalon!' Targesh waved with one hand, a measure

of his growing confidence. 'Ride with me!'

Adalon waved back and shook his head, laughing. 'I have other things to do, Targesh.'

Such as plan what we're going to do next, he thought. Absently, he patted his pockets. One held the magic pipe and another held the set of magic keys. Once they had found that the brass beasts only needed a key to be summoned to life, Adalon had decided to keep the keys together. He'd never carried so much enchantment in his life.

He waved again to Targesh, then turned and went back into the room he had made his own.

They were safe. Adalon knew this should have been enough to make him happy, but it wasn't. A single day in the Lost Castle and he was chafing, looking for an outlet for his Clawed One energy.

He could leap down and run around the courtyard. He shook away that idea. It would only make things worse. It would make the Lost Castle seem like a prison, not a refuge. What good is running if bound by walls?

Adalon walked to the other balcony and gazed across the wall and over the river. The trees were deep and green, beckoning to him.

He knew he could swim the river, then run through the forest, feeling his muscles work and enjoying the wind on his face. He could weave between trees, leap fallen trunks and race through the countryside, head down, tail outstretched for balance.

He sighed. Fun though that may be, he would still be in the Hidden Valley, hemmed in by mountains. He belonged outside.

He had riches enough now, but how was he to use them to fulfil his vow? *Where does one go to buy an army?* he thought, and he idly scratched his name on the balcony with one claw. *What is the first step?*

Metallic clanking and Targesh's grunts of satisfaction made Adalon think of the armoury. He took the magical keys from his pocket and looked at them, feeling their magic. In such a short time, they had found so much. What else could be hidden in such a place? The castle may hold something that would be of more immediate use against Queen Tayesha.

But at what cost? a voice whispered at the back of his mind.

Adalon bowed his head, deep in thought. He

heard his father. '*Wisdom comes in knowing when to act, and when to build strength. Watch, listen, and learn before acting.*'

He knew that three young saur were no match for the might of Thraag, even with the riches they had found. The desire to fulfil his vow burned inside him, but he knew that the time for taking action was not now. This was the time to gather themselves, find allies, explore the wonders of the Lost Castle. *Strike when ready, not when rushed. Let not the hot blood rule the mind*, the Way of the Claw advised.

Adalon nodded, his course clear. Wait, plan, then move with care and stealth. Build strength gradually. Strike when ready.

It was not the course his heart desired, but it was the course that his head said was right.

He glanced at the door and wondered where Simangee was. She had walked her riding beast to the courtyard, but after laughing at Targesh's performance she'd left to explore on her own.

Adalon looked up at the sun. It was nearly midday.

'Canter, steed! Canter!' Targesh's voice echoed from the courtyard. Adalon smiled at his friend enjoying himself so much.

A noise made him turn. Simangee stood in the doorway, shaking, her eyes wide. 'It's begun,' she said, then collapsed.

'Targesh!' Adalon shouted. He thrust the keys into his pocket and hurried to Simangee's side.

Adalon had carried Simangee to her bed by the time Targesh appeared. 'Is she all right?'

'I don't know. Can you get her some water?'

'Aye. Root broth, too.'

'Good.'

Simangee opened her eyes soon after Targesh left. 'I found the chamber of power.' She swallowed and grimaced. 'The book said it would be in a tower. It took me time to find which one.'

'The chamber of power,' Adalon repeated. What was taking Targesh so long?

'Where the A'ak made most of their magic. It has many, many bottles of magic potions. And looking glasses right around the walls.'

'Mirrors?'

'More than mirrors. Through them the A'ak could see what was happening outside this valley. They could spy on all the seven kingdoms.'

'Oh.' Adalon sat up straighter.

'I could not control the mirrors. Their focus swooped and roamed, and would not go where I commanded.' She closed her eyes and tears leaked from them. 'I wanted to find Hoolgar.'

Adalon knew that Simangee respected the old scholar, but until now he had not realised how much. With all the seven kingdoms to see, she had first tried to look for the saur who had taught her.

Her eyes sprang open. 'Sleeto, Adalon, do you remember Sleeto?'

'Yes. Of course.' Adalon's fears for Simangee were renewed. Why was she talking of their childhood playground? Was she delirious?

'The Queen is sending troops to Sleeto. The construction of the great fortress is to begin in earnest. They mean to enslave the villagers and once the citadel is made, the invasion of Callibeen will be launched.'

Adalon closed his eyes for a moment, then opened them again.

Simangee lifted herself up and grabbed Adalon's arm. Her eyes were blazing. 'We must stop them, Adalon.'

She crumpled to the bed.

Adalon stroked her forehead for a moment. Targesh arrived. 'Asleep?' he asked, concern plain on his broad face.

Simangee opened her eyes. 'No. I feel like my bones are made of rubber.'

'The cost of magic,' Adalon muttered. 'Weakness? A small price, this time.'

Simangee nodded and rubbed her crest. 'I will recover. I must.' She looked urgently at Adalon. 'You know what we have to do, don't you?'

Targesh looked from Adalon to Simangee, then back again. 'What is it?'

Adalon told his friend of what Simangee had seen.

Targesh frowned. 'We must save Sleeto.'

'How?' Adalon said. 'What can we do?' He sprang to his feet. 'I want to stop the Queen from destroying not just Sleeto, but all of Thraag – and the other saur nations. If we ride out now, what will we achieve? Quick deaths. We must wait, build our strength, strike when we are strong.'

'Sleeto, Adalon,' Simangee said. 'We must help them.'

Targesh looked at him. 'Loyalty to the herd.' He grunted. 'They're our friends.'

Adalon gazed at both of them, his comrades since childhood. They had saved him from prison and the clutches of Queen Tayesha. They had risked their lives to help him. Now they were asking him to help others. They were selfless – not thinking of their own plight – and it shamed him. They had put his welfare ahead of their own, without complaint and without reproach.

A great truth came to him: sometimes, instead of doing the best thing, one had to do the right thing.

It was not a lesson from the Way of the Claw. Its wisdom had the clarity of the old lessons, but it did not belong in their litany. Where did it come from?

In a moment of insight, he understood it came from within.

'Look after her.' Adalon took the magical keys from his pocket. 'I won't be long.'

Simangee's eyes flew open. 'No! We must all go!'

'Hush,' said Targesh. 'Quiet now.'

'No,' Simangee said. 'We must present ourselves to the cabinet together.'

'Cabinet?' Targesh asked Adalon.

'In the armoury. More magic.'

'Ah.' He looked at Simangee. 'I'll carry you.'

'I can walk,' she said, but when she tried to stand, she stumbled and almost fell.

Targesh put her arm around his shoulder. 'Walk with me.'

Simangee half-smiled. 'All right. A little. But I'm already feeling stronger.'

Adalon stood with his friends in front of the iron cabinet. Simangee looked uncertain, but Targesh sniffed the scent of oil and metal in the armoury. His eyes were bright and keen as his gaze roamed over the racks of weapons.

'Three of us,' Adalon said. 'Three of us against a kingdom. But great oaks grow from small acorns.'

He fitted the iron key into the keyhole and turned it without hesitating. He seized both handles and flung the doors open.

Simangee sighed. Targesh's eyes went wide. Adalon clenched his hands and felt claws bite into his palms.

The cabinet was larger inside than it was outside, stretching into a distance that was lost in haze. Adalon looked again. It wasn't right. The interior of the cabinet was twisted, not square. No, that wasn't it. It was tilted, just a little. He shook his head. That wasn't it either. He turned away for a moment. It hurt his eyes if he looked too long. A smell like hot sand made his nostrils ache.

'Hrmph!' Targesh stamped his feet and snorted. 'More magic.'

'Oh yes,' Simangee said. She rubbed her hands together, and Adalon thought she looked like a youngling gazing at a table laden with sweet pastries. True to her word, it seemed she had recovered from her collapse.

Adalon stepped into the cabinet. To his left were racks of armour. On the right were shields and swords. He looked from side to side. The first armour was plate, made of sky blue metal. On the opposite side of the cabinet was a matching blue shield and sword.

Next in line was green banded armour, the same glittering colour as emeralds. A green shield and a green axe stood opposite.

The third was ruby-red chain mail, with a red shield and a red bow.

After that the arms and armour were grey and shadowy. Adalon reached out for the fourth set but pulled his hand back, hissing. Something stopped his claws, something both hot and cold, burning his skin.

'Green,' Targesh said, rubbing his nose horn. 'I like green.'

'Are you sure it's yours?' Adalon asked.

Targesh smiled and pointed at the green armour, neatly laid out. 'No helmet.'

Adalon nodded. Of course a Horned One would need no helmet. Besides, the green armour looked a perfect fit for Targesh's burly frame.

'The magic has sorted us out,' Simangee said. 'The red bow is mine, I'd imagine. And the red armour.' She lifted the red bow and a curiously designed helmet. It had a cunning hinge that allowed it to fit neatly around Simangee's bony crest. She then drew up a telescoping series of scales. Simangee held out her hands. 'See?'

The ruby-red armour made Simangee look like an exotic bird. Adalon smiled.

He lifted the sky-blue helmet and settled it over his head. It was light, hardly any weight at all. Even though the eyeholes were mere slits, Adalon could see as well as if he wasn't wearing a helmet at all.

'No-one would know who you are,' Simangee said, and her voice came unmuffled to Adalon. 'You look like a hero from the clouds.'

'From legend,' Targesh said, and his words made Adalon shiver.

He turned his head to the left and to the right. The helmet did not impede him in any way. It felt as if he had been wearing it all his life.

'Ready yourselves,' he said. 'We ride to Sleeto.' Adalon seized the sword. Without thinking, he swung it at a nearby bench. All his worry and his frustration were behind the swing, but he was still stunned when the bench was cloven in two.

He held up the sword and stared at it. Targesh clapped him on the back and grinned. 'Powerful magic.'

Adalon only hoped that the cost for such power would not be more than they could pay.

Twenty-three

The great brass riding beasts bounded through the gates of the castle with the clashing of metal. When they reached the river, they stopped.

'Do you have the pipe?' Simangee asked Adalon.

He took it from a pouch on his belt. *If the magic is useful, I can endure the pain*, he decided. He lifted his visor, and blew on the pipe.

A noise like a high-pitched whine set Adalon's teeth on edge, but that was all – and it soon disappeared. No visions came to him. He shook himself and urged his steed over the solid water.

When they reached the perilous exit from the Hidden Valley, Adalon held up a claw. With a clatter like a band putting down their instruments, the riding beasts came to a halt. 'Simangee. As soon as the mountain finishes its roaring, we can pass?'

'Yes. But we mustn't linger.'

The riding beasts were not frightened by the smell of burning rock or the jets of fire. Their clashing hoofs struck sparks as they raced through the tunnel and out onto the mountain's flank.

Adalon's breath was whipped away as they surged down the slope of Graaldon. Behind him he heard Targesh whooping with delight.

The brass riding beasts were tireless. Heading north-east, they galloped through the stony plain, through the grasslands, through the dark forest and through the wild countryside, faster than Adalon had ever gone before. Birds scattered in front of them and wildlife fled. Adalon felt like an arrow in flight as he rode low, eyes squinting against the wind.

After hours of riding, they burst through trees and startled a party of woodcutters. The woodcutters stared open-mouthed at the mirror-bright armour and the metal steeds. Adalon and his companions hurtled through the clearing and vanished into the forest beyond.

The day flew by as the great brass steeds ate up miles with their strides. Adalon rode grimly, his two friends flanking him. He wondered if he should halt to rest, but the determination on the faces of Simangee and Targesh pushed him on. They followed streams and rivers, fording where they could. They rode around villages and hamlets, setting watch beasts barking. They rode on and on.

The mountains called to them, the great ragged Skyhorn Ranges, the border between Thraag and the eastern kingdoms of Callibeen, Shuff and Chulnagh. Perched high in the clouds was Sleeto, the sole pass through the mountains.

Finally, in the broad late afternoon, they came to the foothills and the main road from Challish. It was a dusty trail, barely wide enough for a heavy wagon. It wound its way through woods and up into the heights.

Adalon reined in his great brass steed. He pushed up his visor as his friends circled around him. They all stretched tired muscles. Staunch, brave Targesh was solemn. Simangee looked weary but determined. *Good friends, both of them*, Adalon thought. Yet here he was about to take them into battle where they could be killed . . .

'We must do this,' Simangee said before Adalon could speak. 'How could we not?'

'Yes,' Targesh said. '*Resist. Defend. Repel.* The Way of the Horn.'

In that moment Adalon knew that this friendship was worth all the treasure in the Lost Castle. He slammed down his visor. 'Now, let us ride to Sleeto!'

The road rose steeply. It switched back and forth again and again as it took them toward the gap between the two great peaks. The brass steeds climbed without complaint.

At last, a turn and over a rise, and Adalon held up a hand. Targesh and Simangee reined in close behind him, waiting, silent.

Adalon cocked his head to listen. The sounds of metal on metal came echoing off the mountainside. Shouts and screams mingled with the clangour.

'What is it, Adalon?' Simangee asked, her visor raised.

'Battle. Troops are at Sleeto.'

Targesh sniffed. 'Smoke.'

Adalon urged his steed forward. Together, the three friends thundered along the road to Sleeto.

Twenty-four

Sleeto lay in a small valley. For centuries it had seen travellers and merchants passing from Thraag to Callibeen and beyond. The inn of Sleeto was famous, with beer made from fresh mountain water. It was a peaceful, pretty place and Adalon, Targesh and Simangee had spent many happy times there.

But this day, happiness was a stranger. Adalon stared in horror at the scene below them. Smoke rose from burning buildings, and troops on riding beasts wheeled back and forth.

He could see that the attackers were a light force, barely twenty soldiers. Plenty to deal with such a tiny village in the mountains. The commander hadn't reckoned, however, on the fierce pride of the mountain saur. They hadn't gone peacefully with the troops. They had resisted. At least one soldier was lying face down near one of the houses. But the villagers had fared much worse than the soldiers. Strewn around the small town were what appeared at first glance to be motionless bundles of rags – Adalon shuddered when he realised what they were.

The soldiers were circling the inn, the largest building in the town. The shutters were closed and Adalon knew the villagers would have retreated there for safety.

Adalon drew his sword. Simangee had her bow in hand and had already nocked an arrow. Targesh hefted his axe. Without a word, they plunged toward the troops.

As they raced closer, Simangee released an arrow, then another. In an instant, she had half a dozen ruby-red shafts speeding toward the attackers.

Adalon and Targesh roared. They whirled their weapons and fell on the soldiers.

Simangee's shafts had already sown confusion in the troops. When they saw three mirrored warriors on steeds of brass, they began to panic. They tried to turn their riding beasts to face these new foes, but some went one way, some another. Riding beasts reared, spilling riders; some galloped off despite the cursing of the soldiers.

Before the troops could order themselves, Adalon and Targesh were on them.

Adalon was grim as he dealt with them. It gave him no pleasure, no joy. When he remembered the vision he had had of the A'ak, and the terrible aftermath of battle where death was the only victor, any excitement withered in his chest.

His sword was light in his hand, slashing and hacking, dancing like a sky-blue flame. It split shields and shattered swords. The eyes of Adalon's foes showed terror as he hewed his way through them. They fell back, trying to avoid him.

Targesh was alongside, bellowing and swinging the great green axe as if it were a straw. Any unfortunates who came close enough were flung aside with a toss of his mighty horns.

The brass riding beasts were deadly. They kicked and bit and trampled, clanging with the sound of a giant's foundry.

All around, Simangee's arrows buzzed like angry

red wasps, each finding a target. Adalon felt one hum past as he struck at a rangy Toothed One. It was as if a crimson flower suddenly sprouted in the saur's chest. He fell backward.

In the middle of the battle, Adalon raised his head and saw a crooked figure on a ridge nearby. He tried to see the figure more clearly, but a Plated One loomed up at him. Adalon fended off a mace with his shield, which felt light as a feather. He crashed the shield into the face of his attacker and then peered again at the observer on the ridge.

He was a Toothed One – that was clear – wearing chain mail instead of the plate armour that the rest of the troops wore. It was plain that only chain mail could cover the misshapen body of this saur.

The Toothed One raised a claw and pointed to the right wing of the troops. A dozen riders fell back, then regrouped and charged at Adalon, Targesh and Simangee.

Just as the riders closed on him, realisation came to Adalon with enough force to take his breath away. *Wargrach!*

The saur who had killed his father had not died in the mouth of Graaldon! Fury erupted in Adalon and he spurred his brass steed forward. The red mist of anger began to colour his vision as his sword moved faster and faster. His heart started to swell with the beauty of battle. Every thrust became a song; every parry became a dance. What had he been thinking? Battle was glorious, not grim! Strength, victory, triumph – these were what war was about! He swung his blade over his head, laughing.

At this sight, the remaining soldiers pulled up. 'Come!' Adalon cried. 'All of you! I'll take you all! Then I'll take your leader!' He pointed his sword at Wargrach, who stood, unmoving, on the ridge.

The soldiers turned and fled.

Adalon threw his head back and screamed. How dare they? Running from battle? Cowards! They deserved to die the death of ages!

He went to spur his brass steed on, but Targesh stepped in front of him and seized the bridle. 'No,' the Horned One said.

'Out of my way!' Adalon lifted his sword.

Targesh did not move. He gazed at Adalon.

Stupid Horned One! Adalon thought. *It's time he was taught a lesson!*

He began to bring down the sword and then he

stared stupidly at the arrow that pierced his forearm, neatly through a joint in his armour. The sword dropped from his hand, bounced off the shoulder of his steed and then lay on the ground.

'Take his helmet off, Targesh,' Simangee ordered as she slung her bow over her saddle.

Together, they eased Adalon to the ground. He glared at them and hissed. His tail thrashed at them until Targesh trapped it beneath his knee. 'Unhand me, ingrates! Wargrach is out there. I must take him!'

Simangee held his head and stared into his eyes. 'Let go of the fury, Adalon. The magic armour, the weapons, are drawing on it, stoking it until it consumes you.'

Adalon shook with rage. He wanted his weapons. He wanted to be out there, leading the A'ak to victory, to fulfil their destiny as the rulers of all. Every saur in Krangor would bow down before the A'ak!

Adalon shook his head. *A'ak? What am I thinking?*

That was enough. The rage began to recede, drawing back like the waning tide. 'Simangee?'

'Adalon? Are you yourself again?'

Adalon's heart was hammering in his chest and his head felt light, as if he had not eaten for days. His forearm hurt. 'I thought I was the leader of the A'ak.'

He had wondered at the price for using such magical stuff as the armour and weapons. Now he knew.

'And now?' Targesh rumbled.

Adalon snorted. 'Adalon who was once of the Eastern Peaks.'

'Adalon of the Lost Castle?' Simangee said, grinning. Together, she and Targesh helped him to his feet.

'That may do,' Adalon allowed. 'That may do.'

He held out his arm and stared. An arrow was sticking right through it. The pain, however, was dull – an ache that he could ignore.

Targesh snapped the head off the arrow and, delicately, pulled the remains from Adalon's arm. Simangee took a bandage from a pouch at her belt and bound the wound.

'You are wearing the A'ak armour too. Did you feel nothing?' he asked her. She shook her head. 'Targesh?'

'No.'

Simangee looked up. 'What price will *we* pay for using the armour, Adalon?'

'I don't know. You may escape with something minor, or nothing at all.'

Targesh shrugged. 'My back itches.'

The doors of the inn burst open. To Adalon, it looked as if the whole population of the village flooded out. Males, females, younglings, oldsters, all armed with whatever weapons they had to hand when the soldiers fell on their village – some old swords and axes, but mostly hoes, picks and shovels. The blacksmith grimly carried his largest hammer.

Adalon faced the frightened villagers. 'Bolggo!' he said sharply, searching for the innkeeper. 'It's Adalon!'

A short, burly Plated One pushed through the crowd. He wore an apron and carried a wicked-looking club. 'Adalon?'

'Yes, it's me.'

Targesh and Simangee walked their riding beasts close. Simangee grinned and removed her helmet. 'Any chance of a meal for some weary travellers?'

Twenty-five

Six days later, Wargrach whipped his riding beast along, gritting his teeth against every jolt. He bore the pain, knowing that every step took him further away from the mess at Sleeto. The path he had chosen took him away from Challish, too, and Queen Tayesha.

The riding beast halted at a fork in the way. Wargrach urged it on, taking the route that led deeper into the woods.

Queen Tayesha would not look kindly on losing another cohort of troops. Coming so soon after the disaster at Graaldon, such events looked like carelessness, and that wasn't a good quality in a commander. No, Wargrach knew that this was a good time to keep his distance from the Queen and her plans.

The riding beast was wilting, breathing hard, head hanging low. Wargrach had no pity for it. He needed to get to the top of the next hill and he would almost be at his destination.

To distract himself from his aching body, Wargrach cast his mind back to Sleeto. Who were those metal warriors? What magical power did they possess, fighting like demons as they did? Wargrach's troops were veterans, battle-hardened and experienced. Yet they were scattered by three individuals.

His face grimaced horribly in something that had once been a smile. Their efforts were all for nothing, anyway. Sleeto was not rescued. Its fate was merely postponed. Queen Tayesha was sending out the rest of the force, then another, until the fortress at Sleeto was built – with the help of that weakling Moralon. She was not about to give up on her plans.

Nor was Wargrach. He had suffered setbacks in achieving his dreams, true, but the best commander always had plans behind plans, something to fall back on if necessary.

The riding beast stumbled, and broke through overhanging bushes at the crest of the hill. Wargrach grimaced again and he began to feel a sort of grim happiness.

Below him lay the castle of High Battilon, the stronghold of the Eastern Peaks, the place Wargrach had decided would be his new home.

Queen Tayesha sat on the stone throne. Her arms were on the rough armrests. She could feel her link with the land. It reminded her of her duty and it made her strong.

Standing in front of her were the remaining five generals of the kingdom. All of them were Toothed Ones, all of them experienced, and all of them very nervous.

They had heard of the events at Sleeto, for each of them had their spies. Queen Tayesha appreciated that. They would not have risen to the positions they had if they did not have cunning on their side.

But none of them was Wargrach.

'Generals,' she snapped, 'you have served me

well in the past.' She paused and heard the sound of seven generals breathing again. 'But your challenge is to serve me even better in the future.'

Nothing could tear the generals' attention away from her. They listened keenly because they knew their lives may depend on how well they did it. Queen Tayesha was pleased.

'General Wargrach is no more,' she announced. Some of the commanders showed surprise, a few concern. No-one had heard any details as to what had happened to Wargrach. He had vanished after the events at Sleeto. Most had guessed that the Queen had him put to death.

Two of the generals showed interest, and Queen Tayesha noted that. They were the ones who were already wondering if they could fill Wargrach's position, no doubt. Ambition was a promising trait.

'The invasion of Callibeen must continue without him,' she said. 'You five have the task of mobilising our armies, planning our campaign, and building the fortress at Sleeto. Do not fail me.'

The generals saluted as one, then marched from the Throne Hall, armour and weapons clashing as they went. Queen Tayesha remained.

When they had gone, she put a hand to her forehead and sighed. She felt old. The years she had kept at bay were still there, hovering around her like gnats on a summer's day.

Shouldn't she give up? Without Wargrach it was going to be harder to achieve her dream. Perhaps the moment had come to accept that time was going to win after all.

Queen Tayesha straightened. No, she wasn't about to surrender. It was her *duty* not to surrender. The saur needed her! Their fate was in her hands!

She stood and held her hands up in front of her face. Magic surged from one to the other in a cascade of silver light. 'I will do it,' she announced to the empty Throne Hall. 'I will unite the seven kingdoms of Krangor!'

Twenty-six

Adalon stood on a balcony of the Lost Castle, his arm in a sling. The pain nagged at him, but he ignored it. The courtyard below was filled with the villagers from Sleeto. The savoury smell of vegetable stew and roasting meat came from cooking fires. Children played hide and seek, running up stone staircases and along battlements.

At least they are safe here, Adalon thought. That was the argument that had convinced the villagers to come all this way to the Hidden Valley. Safety. They knew as well as Adalon that the Queen would not let the village rest in peace.

It had been hard for the villagers to leave homes

that had been in their families for centuries. Bolggo the innkeeper finally convinced them. 'Look at me!' he had said. 'If I can leave my inn behind, you can leave your houses!'

It had been Bolggo's idea to set fire to the town. 'The Queen's soldiers won't have the pleasure of using our dwellings,' he spat as he threw the blazing torch onto the thatch of his own inn.

The villagers wept as they marched out of Sleeto. Smoke climbed into the air and hung there for a long time after, so that looking back they could all see where their homes had once been.

A journey that had taken the magic steeds a day took nearly a month for the Sleeto villagers. With children and old ones, the passage was dangerous and slow. Adalon, Targesh and Simangee were kept busy finding food in the great forests of west Thraag, scouting the best paths through the wilderness, and – on three harrowing occasions – doing battle with small bands of soldiers. It was an exhausting, perilous time, but they finally reached the Hidden Valley and safety.

Adalon clicked his claws together. *Safe in an A'ak place?* He still had misgivings about dwelling in the home of the mysterious saur. He felt that there was much still to discover about them.

Simangee and Targesh joined Adalon on the balcony. Targesh was eating skewered vegetables. 'Good cooks, those villagers.'

'What are they going to do?' asked Simangee. 'They can't stay in this courtyard forever.'

Adalon already had a plan. 'They're saur of the land. The abandoned farms in this valley are crying for hands to work them.'

Simangee took the skewer from Targesh and nibbled a piece of roasted pumpkin. With the skewer, she pointed at the innkeeper. 'Bolggo found cellars here in this castle, and a brewing room. He wants to start again.'

'He's welcome,' Adalon laughed.

Adalon, Simangee and Targesh leaned against the balcony and watched the villagers go about their domestic business with a mixture of relief and sadness. They had left behind their homes, but they were still alive and they were safe. Gratitude and loss mingled together and left them feeling off balance, as if each had gone lame in both feet at once.

Adalon thought of the battle of Sleeto. He

remembered the power of the magic sword and the fear in the eyes of the soldiers when they saw the three metal heroes riding toward them. He also remembered the blood lust that overcame him. He knew that was the cost the magic weapons and armour demanded. What was he to do about that? Forswear the weapons, never use them again? The magic of the A'ak was their best hope of thwarting the Queen's plans – could he pay the price for using it?

Some right decisions are simple, others not. Knowing the difference is the key. The lesson of the Way of the Claw came unbidden to him. Lately, he had spent much time contemplating the teachings and had found some solace.

Of course, whenever he brought them to mind, they sounded as if they were spoken by his father. He smiled. It was good to remember him this way.

'I went to the chamber of power this morning,' Simangee said. 'I looked in the mirrors.'

Adalon studied his friend. 'Are you all right?'

She shrugged. 'Just a little tired. I must be getting used to it.'

'What did you see?' Targesh asked.

'I was looking for Hoolgar. We could use his wisdom.'

Adalon agreed wholeheartedly. 'Did you find him?'

'No.'

'See anything else?' Targesh asked.

'Challish. More soldiers, the Army growing.'

'Ready to invade Callibeen,' Adalon said softly.

'What will we do, Adalon?' Simangee said.

'We will fight.' He gazed into a distance that held his enemies, his people and his future. 'It would be wrong not to.'

BOOK TWO

THE MISSING KIN

Read a special preview of *The Missing Kin*, the second book in the Chronicles of Krangor!

The echoing corridors of the Lost Castle held many surprises. Adalon knew that most were dangerous, some deadly, but the urge to explore the vastness of their refuge overwhelmed such considerations.

In the month since Adalon and his friends had returned to the Lost Castle after saving the villagers of Sleeto, he'd taken to wandering the mysterious halls and chambers, pondering the fate of the long gone A'ak. As summer lingered and finally eased into a gentle autumn, he explored the passageways and gazed into room after room, trying to make sense of the enigmatic A'ak. Where were they? Why had they disappeared? What *kind* of saur were they?

One morning, while exploring, Adalon almost overlooked the opening to a narrow spiral staircase, concealed as it was in the ornamental carving that was so common in this part of the castle. It was only when he swung his lantern that the shadows disappeared enough for him to see the stairs leading downwards.

Behind a solid wooden door at the bottom of the stairs was a small square room. The walls were rough stone, most unlike the smoothly finished masonry he'd become accustomed to. The blocks were irregular with uneven faces, as if hastily put together. Three empty niches at shoulder height marked each wall.

A stone door stood opposite, as solid as a mountain. A pile of rocks was heaped next to it, nearly reaching the ceiling, as if bad workers had thrown them aside before slouching off.

Adalon flexed his claws and wrinkled his snout. The air smelled stale and old. It reminded him of the deepest chamber in his ancestral home of High

Battilon. That chamber rested on bedrock, the bones of the land, and it was there that Adalon had made his great vow of vengeance against Queen Tayesha and her cunning and vicious General Wargrach.

A soft *click* came from behind him. Adalon whirled around and saw that the door – which he was *sure* he'd left open – was now shut. He tried to open it, but it wouldn't move. He bared his teeth, alert, eyes darting. He turned and sidled along until he had his back to a wall. He placed the lantern in one of the niches and held his clawed hands wide, ready. Unarmed though he was, his thumb-claws were sharp and deadly. He cursed himself for exploring alone.

At first, his friend Simangee had gone with him on these expeditions. Her singing had echoed down the empty hallways, and rose to the lofty rafters. She was undismayed by dust and darkness; to her, the Lost Castle was a great playground. Despite Adalon's concern, she bounded through doorways, always anxious to see what lay beyond. The melodious burbling that resonated through her bony crest accompanied them as they stumbled on countless rooms full of A'ak furniture and belongings, all arranged as if the owners had merely stepped out for a moment.

But Simangee had tired of exploration. She decided to spend more time high in one of the towers, in the chamber of power she'd found. Adalon had misgivings but she was insistent, pointing out that the many magic potions in the room needed careful investigation if they were to be of use in their struggle against Queen Tayesha.

Adalon had tried to interest Targesh in exploring the castle. The massive Horned One was tempted, but was too busy helping the villagers settle into their new home. So Adalon explored alone. He wasn't altogether unhappy about his solitude. It gave him time to think about their circumstances. Three young saur defying the Queen of Thraag's plans to rule all of Krangor? A futile task, and yet the mysterious artefacts they'd already found in the Lost Castle gave them some hope. The magical armour, weapons and steeds had been vital in defeating Queen Tayesha's soldiers at Sleeto.

Adalon hissed, and cursed himself for letting his mind wander. He narrowed his eyes and scanned the confined space. He felt his heart began to race, and soon his blood was afire. He tried to compose himself, thinking of the principles of the Way of the Claw. When his heartbeat slowed, he tried to open the door again. But it was as solid as the stone walls which surrounded it. Adalon's tail twitched with frustration.

He eyed the door opposite. The great slab of stone was banded with metal. Although it looked primitive, almost crude, it fitted precisely into its frame with only the tiniest gap. He took a careful step towards it, hoping it wouldn't be locked.

Next to the door, the pile of stones moved. Adalon stared, certain he hadn't disturbed it. A pebble tumbled from the top of the pile, bouncing off the larger rocks until it reached the floor, where it skittered along before coming to rest in front of him.

The pile shivered, and larger stones ground together and shifted. Adalon's mouth was dry. It was as if something was trying to get out from under the heap. He snapped his claws together and raised himself on his toes. His heart hammered and then he remembered a lesson from the Way of the Claw: *Do not run the race before it begins*. He searched for stillness inside him and tried to steady himself.

Adalon jumped back as the entire top half of the rock pile lurched and then fell forward. He rose on his toes, but nothing appeared. Cautiously, he took a step toward it.

With a grating sound that set Adalon's teeth on edge, the stones shivered and edged closer, as if dragged by an unseen force. The movement seemed random at first, with stones jostling and scraping against each other, until finally they heaved themselves up in a single mass.

Numb, Adalon saw that the rocks had assembled themselves into the crude figure of a giant saur. It had two arms, two legs, a thick tail and a featureless, rough head that scraped the ceiling.

Adalon shook his head. *Magic*, he thought. *How I loathe magic.*

The stone creature stood still for a moment, then its head swayed, as if it were tasting the air. With a jerky step, it lurched towards him, the floor shaking beneath its foot. Adalon moved to his left, keeping his back to the wall. The creature took another ponderous step. It paused and the stones which made up its body ground together as it settled. Then it swung a massive arm.

Adalon threw himself forward, dodging underneath the deadly blow. He rolled and came to his feet in time to twist away from a backswing that would have torn off his head. He feinted left, then darted right. A rocky fist crashed into the wall, sending splinters of stone spinning. One sliced Adalon's cheek. He wiped blood away and realised he'd barely avoided being blinded.

He lunged, then reeled back as the monster swung its tail. Where was it vulnerable? The stones scraped against each other, nothing presenting itself – no eyes, no soft belly, nothing. Perhaps if he could lure it to one side, he could reach the door it had been guarding.

Adalon sprang toward the monster, then slipped to his right. It tried to grapple with him, clutching with both arms, but Adalon squirmed away with Clawed One speed. He left some skin behind, but the way was now clear to the door.

He raced for it, but at that instant the monster swung its tail again. Adalon tried to stop and duck at the same time, but his feet skidded out from under him. The massive tail clipped his forehead. His head rang from the blow, and he felt as if his bones had turned to liquid. He slid to the floor.

For an instant Adalon lay there, dazed. He knew he should be climbing to his feet, but his thoughts were wrapped in fog. He looked up to see the monster dragging itself around to face him.

Dizzy, his head swimming, Adalon could see his death shambling towards him. His spirits fell. His vow would remain unfulfilled. His father's death would be unavenged, Queen Tayesha would bring war and ruin to the seven kingdoms of Krangor and General Wargrach would be triumphant.

He shook his head. It hurt, but it cleared a little. He was determined not to die lying down. He struggled to his feet to meet his foe.

At that moment the door to the stairwell splintered and burst apart. A torrent of water roared into the room with a thunder that made the stone walls echo.

Adalon was driven backwards by the flood, spluttering and gasping. Amazed, he saw Simangee wade into the room with a glowing potion bottle in one upraised hand and a lantern in the other. 'Adalon!' she cried. 'Get back!'

Simangee, waist deep in water, threw the potion

at the monster. The vial shattered in a ball of light. Adalon shielded his eyes and when he looked again, the creature was melting – slowly at first, then more rapidly, like an ice statue thrust into the midday sun. In a few scant seconds it had lost its shape. Now a grey mound, it slumped and was dissolved into the water.

Adalon stood, blinking and rubbing his head. Simangee waded to his side. 'Adalon,' she said, 'when are you going to learn not to go anywhere dangerous without me?'

About the Author

Michael Pryor has published more than a dozen fantasy books and over forty short stories, from literary fiction to science fiction to slapstick humour. Michael has been shortlisted four times for the Aurealis Awards, nominated for a Ditmar Award and longlisted for the Golden Inky award, and three of his books have been Children's Book Council of Australia Notable Books. Michael is also the co-creator (with Paul Collins) of the highly successful Quentaris Chronicles. He is currently writing *Word of Honour: The Third Volume of The Laws of Magic*, as well as further books in the Chronicles of Krangor series.

For more information about Michael and his books, visit www.michaelpryor.com.au.